"Keir, please don't say no! I *need* this—we both do!"

Just what was going on inside that handsome head of his? For perhaps thirty of the longest seconds of her life Sienna watched and waited. At long last he drew in a deep uneven breath.

"Two conditions..." he said slowly.

"Anything! Anything at all, if you'll just say yes!"

"Condition one..." Keir marked it off on one long finger of his left hand. "We have a proper wedding. All the trimmings. A church ceremony, flowers, candles, the lot."

"Whatever you say. And—and condition two?"

"After the proper wedding we have a real marriage. I won't stand for anything else. For one thing, there's no way we'll convince anyone that this is the love match you're supposed to have by the conditions of your father's will if we don't look really together. It's all or nothing."

All or nothing.

When Sienna desperately offers Keir Alexander a temporary marriage of convenience, he has a surprise proposition of his own—their marriage must be a real one! Talented Harlequin Presents® author Kate Walker takes you on a breathtaking ride of passion and sensuality, as Keir proves to Sienna he will not be content with just being her "hired husband"!

Legally wed,
Great together in bed,
But he's never said...
"I love you."
They're...

Wedlocked!

The series where marriages are made
in haste...and love comes later....

Coming in October 2002

Marriage on Command
by
Lindsay Armstrong

Kate Walker

THE HIRED HUSBAND

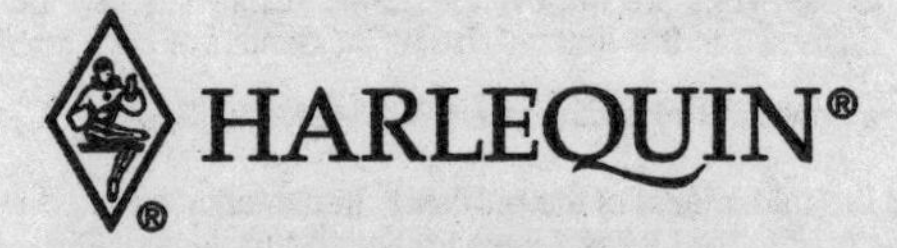

TORONTO • NEW YORK • LONDON
AMSTERDAM • PARIS • SYDNEY • HAMBURG
STOCKHOLM • ATHENS • TOKYO • MILAN • MADRID
PRAGUE • WARSAW • BUDAPEST • AUCKLAND

ISBN 0-373-12275-6

THE HIRED HUSBAND

First North American Publication 2002.

This edition published by arrangement with Harlequin Books S.A.

Visit us at www.eHarlequin.com

Printed in U.S.A.

CHAPTER ONE

'YOU want *what*?'

His expression said it all, Sienna reflected unhappily. He didn't have to speak a single word. Shock, disbelief and sheer antipathy to her suggestion were stamped clearly onto Keir Alexander's hard features, leaving her in no doubt as to how he felt.

'You want what?' he repeated now, the edge in his voice sharpening on every word as his deep brown eyes glared into her anxious blue-green ones.

'I—I want you to marry me.'

It sounded so much worse the second time around. Starker, more incredible, more impossible. She couldn't believe she'd ever had the nerve to ask him once, let alone manage to reiterate her request in the face of his reaction.

If she could have taken it back she would have done so at once, but she had no alternative. She'd tried every other approach, considered every possible answer, but none of them would work. It was Keir or no one. He was her last chance; and if he didn't agree to help her then she was lost. Finished.

'No way, lady!' It was hard, inflexible, adamant. 'No way at all.'

'But—'

'I said *no*!'

'But, Keir…'

But she was talking to the back of his head, and a moment later to empty air as the door slammed to behind him. Keir had walked out on her, rejecting her and her proposal outright, not even sparing her a backward glance. Closing her eyes in despair, her sigh a deep, helpless sound of defeat, Sienna sank down into the nearest chair.

So what did she do now? she asked herself, shaking her dark head despondently. There was nothing she *could* do. No answer presented itself. No fairy godmother appeared to wave her magic wand and put everything right. When she opened her eyes everything was the same as before, the future stretching ahead dark, bleak and with no light at the end of the tunnel.

It had been the worst year of her life so far, and it was still only July. First Dean, and then the loss of her job as an aromatherapist when the beauty salon in which she had worked had closed down. That had been followed by the discovery that her mother, who had clearly been unwell for some time, was in fact suffering from multiple sclerosis. And then, to cap it all, the landlord who owned the small flat she and her mother rented had informed them that he was selling the building. The new owners planned to turn it into a set of offices and they would have to move out—soon.

Oh, it wasn't fair! Sienna slammed one fist into the palm of the other hand in a gesture of frustration and distress. Her mother had to have a home. Somewhere she could live in the comfort and security she needed. The perfect place was available—was hers for the asking. But only if she could meet the conditions laid down. And with Keir's rejection of her proposal her last chance of doing that had been destroyed. She doubted if she would ever see him again.

She didn't know how long she sat there, lost in her misery. She had no idea how much time had passed before the sound of the doorbell pealing through her flat jolted her out of her unhappy reverie. At first she was tempted to ignore it, but when it became obvious that whoever was outside had put their finger firmly on the button and intended keeping it there until they got a response, she forced herself to her feet, dashing down the stairs and wrenching open the door.

She couldn't believe the sight that met her eyes. Keir Alexander stood on the doorstep, dark head held high, his jaw tight, every muscle in his tall, strong body taut with resistance.

'All right,' he said, his voice cold and hard as a sharpened knife. 'Start talking—convince me.'

Sienna talked as she never had in her life before. She couldn't believe that she'd been given a second chance, but she was going to grasp it with both hands, do everything she could—*anything* she could—to ensure it didn't get away from her.

'I know this isn't the way either of us would have done this,' she began, even as they were still climbing the stairs to the first floor where she and her mother lived. 'Not in an ideal world, anyway. It's certainly not the way I ever dreamed of marrying, but beggars can't be choosers. It's the only way I can think of for getting out of a very tight corner indeed, and if you don't agree to help then there's no one else I can turn to.'

She couldn't look at him as she led him into the small sitting room that he had stormed out of such a short time before, painfully conscious of the fact that it was only a few short weeks since the first occasion on which he'd visited her home. Just two months or so since the party at which they'd met.

'You know how ill my mother is—and that it can only get worse. I need to find somewhere for us to live so that I can look after her properly, so…'

'So naturally you want your father's house?' Keir put in harshly.

'Yes.'

Sienna's voice was low and shaken, still carrying the echoes of the way she had felt when a solicitor had contacted her out of the blue. She had been stunned to discover that her father, the man who had abandoned her mother before Sienna had even been born, had had a belated attack of conscience and decided to acknowledge her as his daughter.

As his wife had died some years before, and he had had no other children, he had left her everything he owned in his will. But there was a catch.

'If my—if Andrew Nash hadn't left me all that money, I don't know what I'd have done. And if he hadn't put in the condition, then I wouldn't be forced to involve you in this.'

At last she turned to face Keir, her heart quailing as she saw the heavy lids that hooded his eyes, hiding his thoughts from her. His hands were pushed deep into the pockets of his dark trousers, his shoulders stiff, his very stance declaring hostility and opposition to everything she said.

'The condition being that you have to be married, I presume?'

'That's right. In his letter he said that he'd lived his life wishing he'd chosen differently all those years ago. That he'd realised too late that the love my mother and I could have brought him as a family was more important than the wealth he kept by staying with his wife. And so he made it a prerequisite of my inheritance that I had to be married—happily married—before I could inherit.'

'*Happily* married,' Keir echoed cynically. 'And who's to be the judge of that?'

'My…'

Sienna couldn't get her tongue round the word 'uncle'. After twenty-five years of believing she had no family at all, it was too much to accept that she now had an uncle, particularly one who held her future so securely in his hands.

'His brother, Francis Nash, is to have the final say in seeing that his wishes are carried out. But he knows nothing about me. He's never even seen me. It shouldn't be too hard to—to convince him that… that…'

'That you and I are madly in love and desperate to get married?' Keir finished for her when she couldn't complete the sentence.

'That's right.' It was barely more than a whisper and once more her eyes skittered away from the coldly assessing stare that fixed her like a specimen on a laboratory slide, awaiting analysis. 'W-would you like a drink? There's wine…'

'I think I'd better keep a clear head for this,' Keir returned dismissively. 'I wouldn't want anything to muddle my thinking.'

Did that mean he was actually *considering* the idea? Sienna didn't dare to allow the thought to enter her mind.

'So you want me to play the devoted groom?'

He made it sound like the most repellent task possible. As if he would rather put a gun to his head—anything other than what she had asked of him.

'To lie? Don't you know that lies have a nasty habit of breeding more lies? Before you've time to think you're tangled up in them so tightly that you can't get free and they're dragging you down…'

'But we're not going to lie! Not really. People already know us as a couple. We've been seen out together often enough. It wouldn't be all that different from what we have now. It *wouldn't*!' she declared vehemently when he expressed his disagreement in a harsh sound of disbelief. 'You're here almost every night as it is. What if I'd asked you to move in with me?'

'I'd think you were taking a lot for granted, lady.'

'Keir, it's only supposition!' Desperately Sienna tried to make up the ground she realised she'd lost. 'We both know that our relationship isn't on that sort of footing—that it will probably never be. But we're the only ones who know that. And what we do have is good, isn't it?'

Keir's stony face gave her no encouragement and it was all that she could do not to give up in despair.

'If we decided to say, after a year, that we knew it wasn't working, then we could split—both go our own ways—and it wouldn't matter. There'd be no frayed ends, no regrets, no complications.'

'But this arrangement comes weighed down with complications,' Keir pointed out with cold reason. 'It can't not do that. A marriage certificate complicates things, darling.'

'But it's only a temporary solution, you must see that!' she pleaded with him. 'It won't mean anything to either of us, so you needn't worry about getting trapped in something you don't want! There'll be no commitment beyond that one year—just a twelve month period and then we'll go our separate ways.'

'You make it sound so simple...'

'It *is* simple! It couldn't be anything else. After all, it's not as if you're madly in love with me, or vice versa. And...'

Her voice faded into silence as Keir snatched his hand away from her and moved to stare out of the window, affecting an intent interest in the cars going by in the street.

'It might work,' he said slowly.

Was it possible that he was going to agree? Sienna was past knowing whether she hoped for his agreement or feared it dreadfully. She was so caught up in her own disturbed thoughts at the prospect that she jumped like a startled cat when he suddenly whirled round to face her.

'And what, exactly, would I get out of the deal? Because I presume you were going to offer me something—some remuneration for my co-operation, some compensation for the loss of my freedom by entering into this agreement.'

'Of course.'

Sienna swallowed hard. She had expected this. Had known it must come inevitably. But she hadn't thought he would be quite so cold-blooded about it.

You fool! her heart reproached her. What had she expected? That he would declare that of course he would do it, that he would do whatever she wanted and not expect anything in return?

Of course not. She had known she would have to offer Keir something in exchange for his agreement to help her out. It was just that she hadn't been prepared for the way his demand made her feel that it was that compensation that mattered and not her.

'So?' Keir prompted harshly when she couldn't find the voice to answer him.

'You—you remember what you told me about the shares in Alexander's?'

She had been frankly surprised that he had opened up about so much of his life to her. Keir was the sort of man who kept things very much to himself, limiting the conversation only to uncomplicated, unemotional topics that didn't call for much involvement on either part.

But just three nights earlier he had revealed something of the problems he had been having with the haulage and transportation company of which he was part owner and managing director. Problems that had been caused by his stepmother, his late father's second wife.

Alexander's was a family firm. Originally owned by Keir's father, Don, it had been an ailing, small-scale enterprise when, at twenty-one and fresh from university, Keir had taken it by the scruff of the neck and dragged it forcibly into the late twentieth century. In the following twelve years he had turned it into a huge international success. It was now impossible to travel anywhere in Europe or beyond without seeing one of Alexander's distinctive red and green vehicles somewhere *en route*.

'Did you manage to raise the amount you needed to buy your stepmother out?'

Keir's expression gave her the answer before he spoke, a dark cloud of anger shadowing his face.

'I raised it, but then she upped the stakes again. She says she has another potential buyer in the offing. If that sale goes through then Alexander's as a family firm will cease to exist.'

'And that's so important to you?'

The look her turned on her scorched her from head to toe with its impatient contempt for the stupidity of her question.

'Alexander's is mine, Sienna—*mine*! I'm not prepared to see it the subject of some hostile take-over and swallowed up, becoming just part of another company. I promised my father that, and I'll keep my promise if it kills me.'

'But if your stepmother keeps asking for more?'

Keir's scowl was blacker than ever.

'She knows how much I've invested in modernising things—buying new vehicles, computers, everything over the past year. Given time, that investment will pay off, several hundredfold, but right now it's stretched me to my limit. And Lucille knows that, damn her!'

'How much time would you need?'

'Twelve months, maybe less...'

Sienna knew almost to the exact second the moment that realisation dawned. She saw the subtle changes in his expression, and those dark, knowing eyes slid to her own face, fixing on it in intent appraisal.

'*That's* what you're offering.'

It was a statement, not a question, absolute conviction ringing in his tone, and she could almost hear his astute brain working, weighing up pros and cons, subjecting the idea to shrewd and careful analysis.

'Keir, my inheritance will make me wealthy beyond my wildest dreams. I'll have more than enough to keep myself and my mother in comfort. And I'll be able to help you out too. Oh, *don't* say no!'

He was going to. She knew it just by looking at him. And now that what she hoped for, what she'd prayed might happen, was actually within reach, she couldn't believe that fate would be unkind enough to snatch it away again, right at the last minute.

'Keir, please don't say no! You can pay me back if you like. But I can give you the money you need, and you can help me. I *need* this—we both do!'

Just what was going on inside that handsome head of his? What was that keen, calculating brain thinking? She felt like the accused in some terrible trial. As if she was standing in the dock with Keir acting as both judge and jury, very definitely counsel for the prosecution, about to attack her verbally.

For perhaps thirty of the longest seconds of her life she watched and waited. Watched him consider, debate with himself, accept certain ideas, then just as swiftly reject them. At long last he drew in a deep, uneven breath.

'Two conditions. . .' he said slowly.

'Anything! Anything at all, if you'll just say yes!'

'Condition one...' Keir marked it off on one long finger of his left hand. 'We have a proper wedding. All the trimmings. A church ceremony, flowers, candles, the lot.'

'Whatever you say.'

It was almost impossible to get the words out. Her pulse was racing so fast that her heart seemed to pound against her ribcage, leaving her unable to breathe properly or keep her voice in any way steady.

'And—and condition two?'

'After the proper wedding we have a real marriage. I won't stand for anything else. For one thing, there's no way we'll convince anyone that this is the love-match you're supposed to have by the conditions of your father's will if we don't look really together. It's all or nothing.'

All or nothing. Almost from the moment that they had met she had known that Keir wanted their relationship to be a physical one. He had made no secret of the desire he felt for her, and she had been the one trying to apply the brakes. 'Trying' being the operative word, she acknowledged uncomfortably.

Because she couldn't deny the effect he had on her. From the first moment that he had kissed her, an irresistible, potently sensual chemistry such as she had never known before had sparked between them. It had swept her off her feet, turned her world upside down, taking with it every long-held belief she had ever had about who she was and how she behaved.

It was all the more difficult to cope with because she had never felt like this with Dean. Dean whom she had loved, believed in, trusted. Dean to whom she had given her heart, but even then had never felt the same dangerous, wild excitement that Keir could inspire with simply a look, a touch, a brief caress. She had never understood how she could feel that attraction for a man she barely knew, let alone cared for in the deepest sort of sense.

But perhaps that same excitement would be the saving of her now. Perhaps the unnerving response she felt towards Keir would be enough to turn the fiction of a marriage she was proposing into something that would convince all observers it was actually fact.

But that still didn't make it easy to answer. Her throat closed over a knot of powerful emotions so that all she could do was nod silently, unable to speak a word.

'You agree?' Keir demanded, still in Grand Inquisitor mode.

'I—I agree.'

It was only as she forced it out that comprehension dawned, bright and vivid, blinding her with its brilliance.

She couldn't believe it. Could it possibly be true?

'A proper wedding!' she gasped, struggling to collect what remained of her scattered thoughts. 'A real marriage after a proper wedding! Keir—do you mean—are you agreeing to my proposal?'

The look he turned on her had such a scorching intensity that it seemed to sizzle through the air, sending electrical impulses along every nerve in her body. It spoke of hunger and conquest and passion. But most of all it was redolent with a desire so carnal it seemed positively indecent in the cold light of day.

'Yes, Sienna.'

Hearing his voice, Sienna blinked in disbelief. Suddenly that blazing sensuality was gone, wiped from his face as if it had never been. His tone was emotionless, totally controlled, as blank and indifferent as his eyes, which could have been carved from dark marble they were so cold and lifeless.

'Yes, I'm agreeing to your proposal. Under those conditions, then, yes, I will marry you.'

CHAPTER TWO

'WELL, we did it!'

Sienna's voice was breathless with a mixture of triumph, relief and something coming very close to panic that she prayed the man beside her wouldn't be able to detect. The same emotions were mirrored in the sea-coloured brilliance of her eyes as she turned on him a smile edged with a tension that, try as she might, she was unable to erase completely.

'We did it,' Keir echoed gravely, no answering smile lighting the darkness of his own gaze as it locked with hers. 'But did we get away with it? That's the real question.'

'Oh, don't be silly!'

Sienna made the reproof as careless as was possible when her heartbeat and breathing refused to settle down into anything like their normal rhythm.

'Of course we *got away* with it! Why wouldn't we? And don't say that—you make it sound as if we've done something wrong.'

'And we haven't?'

At his tone, the precarious euphoria that had buoyed her up evaporated in a rush, leaving her feeling disturbingly limp and deflated, like a pricked balloon.

'No, we haven't!' Infuriatingly, she couldn't give the words the conviction she wanted; a quaver she couldn't suppress took all the certainty from her declaration.

'Are you so sure of that? There are those who might label what we've done as fraud, or at the very least an attempt to swindle money from the Nash estate.'

'I'm not swindling anyone! I *am* a Nash, remember? By blood, at least, if not by name. And the only person who might feel defrauded of anything is my father, or rather he might if he was still alive. But, seeing as he never took any interest in my existence from the day I was born, I very much doubt that anything I do now is going to trouble him in the least.'

Moving impulsively, she laid a hand on Keir's arm, her fingers white against the deep colour of his superbly tailored suit as she looked up into the hard-boned strength of his face.

'Don't tell me you're having second thoughts at this late stage?'

'Not second thoughts, no.' Keir pushed one strong hand through his hair, ruffling its gleaming darkness. 'But if we're strictly honest we are pulling a fast one on all those people in there.'

A slight inclination of his head indicated the door at the far side of the room through which the buzz of a hundred conversations could easily be heard.

'Especially your mother.'

'It's because of my mother that I'm doing this,' Sienna reminded him in a vehement undertone made necessary by the need to avoid being heard as the door swung open, revealing the crowded room beyond. 'And you—'

But there was no chance to finish the sentence, because at that moment a loud, stentorian voice broke through the noise, silencing it immediately.

'Ladies and gentlemen—pray silence for the bride and groom!'

'Oh, Lord!'

Taken by surprise, Sienna lurched into a nervous flurry of activity. A hasty glance in the huge, ornately framed mirror over the fireplace reassured her that her veil was still securely anchored, the delicate silver headdress holding it firmly in place in the brown curls of her hair, a couple of shades darker than Keir's.

Her make-up, carefully applied some four hours before, was still almost perfect: a soft wash of beige shadow emphasising the almond shape of her eyes, the long, thick lashes enhanced by a single coat of black mascara. Perhaps the warm pink on the full softness of her mouth had faded just a little, and there seemed to be a surprising lack of colour across the high, slanting cheekbones, but there was nothing she could do about that now. She could only hope that their guests would put her pallor down to excitement or belated wedding nerves.

Patting her cheeks lightly, in an attempt to bring some blood to the surface of her skin in order to make its ivory tones look a little healthier, she turned back to Keir. Meeting his darkly watchful gaze, she switched on what she hoped was a convincing smile, supremely conscious of the fact that it was distinctly ragged round the edges.

'Ready?' he asked, and held out his hand to her.

Sienna could only manage an inarticulate murmur that might have been agreement as she smoothed down her long skirt with uncertain fingers. Made of the finest lace over a delicate silk lining, the dress had originally been her grandmother's, worn on her wedding day almost fifty-five years before. Carefully preserved, wrapped in tissue paper to protect it from the yellowing effects of the light, it had been handed down from mother to daughter in the hope that wearing it as a bride would pass on something of the love that had made the older woman's marriage such a happy one.

But for Sienna's mother, Caroline, there had been no such happy ending. There hadn't even been a wedding ceremony, her daughter reflected bitterly. Her father had already been married. He had had no intention of leaving his wife for the naïve twenty-two-year-old who had been foolish enough to let herself get pregnant as the result of what had, to him at least, been just a pleasant holiday dalliance, with no commitment whatsoever.

'Sienna...' A note of reproof sharpened the edge of Keir's voice, dragging her from her reverie. 'Our guests are waiting.'

The hand he held out moved imperiously, the gesture demanding her instant obedience. For a brief moment the idea of rebellion flared in her mind, but almost immediately she dismissed it.

For now she had to observe all the conventions, play up to everyone's belief that this was the love match of the century. Keir and Sienna, second only to Antony and Cleopatra, or Cathy and Heathcliff in the lists of the all-time great love stories.

Out there, in the elegant dining room beyond the great double doors, was Francis Nash, her late father's brother and only surviving relative. If he was not convinced by their marriage and the whirlwind romance that had apparently preceded it, then the game was well and truly up. One false move and her chance of making sure that her mother spent the rest of her days in the comfort and security she so needed would be ruined.

And so she forced herself to smile again, with rather more success this time, drawing herself up to her full five foot nine as she placed her hand in Keir's.

'I'm ready,' she declared. 'Let's go.'

Hard fingers closed tightly over hers, though whether in encouragement or warning not to take any more risks she couldn't be sure.

'Come on, then,' Keir said, his voice unexpectedly roughened and tight. 'Let's get this show on the road.'

Not giving her time to think, he swung her round and, with her hand held high between them, marched her forcibly across the room, leaving her with no option but to follow him. It was either that or be dragged embarrassingly in his arrogant wake.

In the doorway Keir stopped suddenly, dark head held high, deep brown eyes scanning the elegantly dressed crowd before him as a murmur of interest greeted their appearance. Surprised by his unexpected stillness, it was all Sienna could do to avoid cannoning into the broad, straight line of his back.

Automatically her free hand came out to balance herself, closing over the tight muscles in his arm as she came to an uncertain halt at his side.

'Perfect,' Keir murmured softly, threading the word through with a dark cynicism that she had never heard from him before. 'Now we look just like the model bride and groom on the top of that ridiculously over-decorated cake you insisted on.'

'I...' Sienna began but her muffled protest was ignored as Keir, having caught the eye of the waiting *maître d'*, gave a swift, curt nod as a signal to proceed with the reception.

'Ladies and gentlemen...may I present to you Mr and Mrs Keir Alexander?'

But that was too much. Sienna's head came up sharply, turquoise eyes flashing repudiation of the announcement.

'Mr Keir Alexander and Sienna Rushford!' she pronounced, against the flurry of applause that had greeted the announcement. 'I—'

But the rest of her words were silenced, forced back down her throat, as, with a muttered expletive, Keir caught her in his arms, hauling her up against him as his dark head lowered, his mouth coming down hard on hers.

'Keir!'

His name was a spluttered sound of protest against his lips. It was all she could manage before he kissed her again, with even more ruthless determination.

'Looks like Keir's got a tiger by the tail, all right.'

On the borders of her awareness Sienna heard one of Keir's adolescent stepbrothers make the comment in an aside that was obviously meant to be heard, pitched as it was in a tone that carried clearly in spite of its apparent restraint. The malicious amusement in his voice was impossible to miss.

'Let's hope he's not bitten off more than he can chew.'

Against her slender length Sienna felt the tension that stiffened Keir's hard frame, tightening every muscle into an unyielding wall that seemed to bruise her just to be pressed close to it. So it was almost impossible to equate what all her senses were telling her with the apparently sensual indolence with which he slid his mouth away from hers, trailing it softly over her cheek until his warm breath teased the delicate curves of her ear.

'Do you want this to work or not?' he whispered silkily, his words meant for her hearing alone.

'Of course...'

'Then kiss me!'

'Keir...?' Confusion clouded her eyes, made her voice just a shaken thread of sound.

'Kiss me!'

With a raw, uncontrolled sound in his throat, he closed hard fingers over her chin, wrenching her face up to his once more. But this time when his mouth touched hers it was with an unexpected, beguiling gentleness, a voluptuous tenderness that made her senses swim, her heartbeat slow to a heavy, languorous thud.

Against her back, the strength of his arm was all that held her upright. Without its support she felt that she would melt away completely, sliding into a warm, honeyed pool at his feet. Her whole body glowed, heating the blood in her veins until she felt as if she was flooded with molten gold, a burning spiral of very primitive need uncoiling deep inside her. She wanted to feel Keir's mouth all over her skin, not just on her mouth; she longed for the caress of his hands on parts of her body too intimate to be appropriate on this public occasion.

It had been like this from the start, she acknowledged hazily with the little rational thought that was left to her. With Keir she no longer knew herself. She became a stranger even in her own eyes. In her place was a woman who had her own slender height, delicate oval face and thick fall of long dark brown hair, but who acted in ways she had never seen before.

That Sienna rushed into situations that only months before she would have fled from, screaming in panic.

Situations like this travesty of a marriage that was only for show, with no real foundation in fact.

It was several long drawn-out seconds before the realisation that what she had believed to be distant thunder, or even the crazed pounding of her heart echoing inside her head, was in fact another, louder round of appreciative applause from their audience. A couple of the younger guests even added enthusiastic wolf whistles to the chorus of approval.

With carefully feigned reluctance, Keir broke the embrace and turned a slightly rueful smile on her heated face. To the onlookers, it must have appeared quite genuine, but Sienna had sensed the careful judgement that had had him ending the kiss the full space of several heartbeats before he'd lifted his head. She had seen the calculating look he had directed into her glazed eyes, the triumphant twist to that wide mouth as it had abandoned hers, leaving her aching for more.

Straightening fully, Keir slung a possessive arm around her waist as he turned to face the assembly of friends and relations.

'I'm afraid my wife—' a chorus of cheers greeted his use of the word for the first time since the completion of the marriage ceremony '—has strong feminist views that mean she insists on using her own name instead of adopting mine. Some of you may find that rather unromantic, but personally I have no problem with it. After all, when she indulges my every whim in everything apart from this…'

A careful emphasis on the words 'my every whim' left no room for doubt as to exactly what other things he had in mind.

'Who am I to deny her this one wish for independence if it means so much to her?'

Milking the situation for all it was worth, he smiled down into Sienna's flushed face, his appearance to all intents and purposes every inch that of the doting husband.

'Don't be embarrassed, darling,' he reproved softly.

'You're amongst friends here. Everyone knows how we feel about each other.'

Struggling against a crazy desire to kick him hard on the ankle, in order to let him know exactly how she felt about the charade he was acting out, Sienna forced herself to swallow down the anger she couldn't afford to reveal. Painfully conscious of Francis Nash, standing just a few feet away from her, watching Keir's fooling with an intently speculative air, she managed a rather sickly smile.

But she knew that the curve of her lips wasn't matched by the look in her eyes, which were flashing furious reproof and a warning of later retribution into Keir's mocking face. He really was taking things way too far. Nothing like this had been mentioned in their agreement.

But Keir appeared totally unmoved by the silent rage in her eyes. Instead, taking advantage of the fact that a waiter carrying a tray full of glasses of champagne had just come within reach, he appropriated one of the crystal flutes and held it aloft, dark eyes smiling knowingly down into hers all the time.

'If you'll indulge me,' he declared to the surrounding audience, 'I'd like to propose a toast. To Sienna—my beautiful bride, and the woman who has made me the happiest man in the world by becoming my wife today.'

The man really was incorrigible! In spite of herself Sienna found it impossible to hold back a disturbed squawk of protest at this blatant lie. If Keir didn't stop, someone was going to see right through his over-the-top performance and so start to wonder what the real truth was.

'Keir!' she protested softly, knowing that any further show of anger or impatience would only make him worse, drive him to even more dangerous extremes. 'You're embarrassing me.'

Immediately he was apparently all repentance.

'I'm sorry, darling. You're right. There's a time and a place for this, and that's not here and now. We'll finish later...' Deliberately he let his voice drop a couple of octaves, so that it became a husky purr, rich with sensual promise. 'When we're alone.'

Which earned him yet another cheer of enthusiastic appreciation from the spectators, all of whom completely misunderstood the reasons behind the burning colour that suddenly flooded the bride's face.

'I'll look forward to that,' she shot back in swift retaliation. 'But for now we have our guests to see to. Please, everyone—help yourselves to drinks. I'm sure you're ready for them. Lunch will be served in half an hour. In the meantime…'

She directed her attention back to Keir, her voice and her expression hardening as she did so.

'I think you and I had better circulate—talk to a few people… I'll take this half of the room…'

She had nerved herself for further play-acting on his part, perhaps even a downright refusal to do as she asked, but surprisingly it didn't come. Instead Keir simply lifted his glass in a silent, mocking toast before turning and strolling off in the opposite direction from the one she had indicated.

Silently Sienna watched him go, small white teeth worrying at the fullness of her lower lip as she did so. It would all have been so much easier if she could have been in love with Keir, even just a little. After all, that shouldn't have been too hard. He was the sort of man almost any woman with red blood in her veins would have fallen head over heels for. Tall, strong, impossibly good-looking, with the sort of potent hardcore sexuality that turned susceptible female brains to jelly, leaving them incapable of thought.

He was successful too. A self-made man. A man she could be proud to have at her side, proud to call her husband even for such a strictly limited time. But he would never have her heart. That wasn't hers to give. She had already lost it to someone who had proved every bit as unworthy of her love as her father had been of her mother's lifelong devotion.

No, she mustn't think about Dean. Sienna's teeth dug in

harder as she fought against the tears that burned in her eyes. She had thrown in her lot with Keir, and that was the way her future lay—at least for the term of their contract together. It was an arrangement that she had been convinced could work so well for both of them. But today Keir had behaved in a way she'd never seen before.

Sienna's sea-coloured eyes went to where Keir stood, his dark head thrown back, his face alight with laughter at something his companion had said to him. Suddenly she was brought up hard against the truth of just how very little she actually knew about this man who was now her husband.

If looks could kill, Keir thought wryly, catching that turquoise glare from the opposite side of the room, then he would surely have fallen down dead right on the spot, shrivelled into ashes by the force of Sienna's anger. She hadn't liked his teasing earlier, and clearly the thought of it still rankled. He hadn't realised just how volatile his new wife's temper could be.

His *wife*. Carefully he tested the word inside his mind, not yet sure exactly how he felt about it.

'Keir!' A powerful handshake was accompanied by a hearty slap on the back from a tall man with a bushy dark beard and laughing hazel eyes. 'Congratulations, mate! I never thought I'd see the day that you joined the ranks of married men. This Sienna really must be some woman.'

'Believe me, she is.'

Keir could only pray that his words didn't sound as insincere spoken out loud as they did inside his head. Richard Parry had been his friend for over twenty years now, ever since they had first met up at secondary school, and if anyone was likely to smell a rat at his sudden decision to marry then Rick was that person.

'She has to be. I was really beginning to wonder if you were married to that company of yours. You seemed to spend every waking hour of your life in the office.'

'There have been some problems.' The muscles in Keir's jaw tightened, making his reply sound clipped and distant.

'My father's death was so unexpected that it left a lot of things unresolved…'

'But that was—what?—eighteen months ago? Surely you've sorted things out now?'

'Just about.' Keir nodded slowly, his eyes darker than ever as he thought back over the past year and a half. 'There's one last complication I have to deal with, and then everything will be just how I want it.'

In his business world at least. His personal affairs were quite a different matter. But right now all he could think of was the relief that that one 'complication' had been lifted from his shoulders. It had been the bane of his life for ten years, and he hadn't been able to wait to see the back of it. Only now did he feel free to turn his attention fully to the vexed question of his reckless marriage.

'And when can we expect to hear of a whole new generation of Alexanders?' It was Richard's wife who spoke, her voice soft and gentle as her nature, bringing her husband's head round to her at once.

'Give the poor lad a break, Jo! He's barely put the ring on her finger! Let him at least enjoy the honeymoon before you wish the joys of parenthood on him. Not everyone wants to be plagued with the sort of brood we've got.'

The laughter in Richard's voice was belied by the way his eyes lingered on the swell of his wife's stomach, evidence of how close he was to becoming a father for the fourth time.

'But you always said you wanted children, didn't you, Keir? And I think you'd make a wonderful father—if the way you get on with Sam, William and Hannah is anything to go by.'

'Your children are like their mother, Joanna.' Keir smiled. 'They'd get on with anyone at all without any trouble. But I don't think you should look for the chance of a couple of playmates for your gang at any time in the near future. Sienna and I haven't even talked about having kids…'

What would be the point when this charade of a marriage

they had embarked on wasn't meant to last much longer than a full-term pregnancy anyway? But he couldn't admit that to Rick and Joanna, who were so blissfully happy in their own union that they would find it hard to understand the convoluted reasoning that had led to his taking Sienna as his bride.

'Now if you'll excuse me…I'd better rejoin my wife.'

Coward! Keir reproved himself as he turned away and began to weave a path through the crowd to where Sienna stood on the opposite side of the room, pausing occasionally to shake a hand, acknowledge congratulations and good wishes. But his mind wasn't on what he was doing. He knew he couldn't have faced any more of Joanna's gentle questioning without blurting out something that might have given the game away completely.

The trouble was that Rick and his wife had known him for too long. They had been there all those years before when, under the influence of rather more wine than had been wise, he had declared with impassioned certainty that he would never marry unless he knew it was for ever. That only the conviction that the relationship would last for a lifetime, nothing less, would get him up the aisle and put a ring on his finger.

So how had he ended up doing just that, in the certain knowledge that what he had entered into was just a temporary contract? Stopping dead abruptly, Keir looked down at the thick gold band now encircling his wedding finger, twisting it round and round in an uneasy movement. How come he had compromised all his ideals in this way?

Because he was so much older now—and he would say wiser. He knew that such ideals were nothing but fantasies, impossible to achieve. He had been hit over the head with a strong dose of reality that had driven all the dreams from his mind. These days he was realist enough to know that sometimes a pragmatic compromise was the best you could come away with.

'Keir, darling, I'm so glad to see you…'

This time the hand on his arm was much smaller, finer, totally feminine. Adorned with an extravagant display of gold and diamonds, the slender fingers were tipped with long, pointed nails painted in a violent shade of red. As Keir stiffened instinctively a wave of some heavy, musky perfume assailed his nostrils, turning his stomach.

He would recognise that overpowering perfume anywhere, just as he would recognise the sound of her voice and that false-toned 'darling' that they both knew she didn't mean in the slightest. She only used it for the benefit of everyone else around, in order to maintain the illusion—in reality they had never felt anything other than total hatred for each other.

'Lucille.' He bit the word out, her name leaving a foul, bitter taste in his mouth.

Lucille Alexander. The stepmother from hell and his own personal demon. The woman he had described with deliberate understatement as the one last 'complication' he'd had left to deal with in order to be free of all the problems that had been weighing him down over the past ten years. The woman whose greedy demands had forced him into this marriage that was not a marriage but a purely business arrangement.

And as he turned slowly to face her the wave of revulsion he couldn't control left him in no doubt that the prospect of getting her out of his life once and for all made the pretence and subterfuge totally worthwhile.

CHAPTER THREE

'IS SOMETHING wrong?'

'Wrong?'

Keir's voice was distracted, his attention obviously elsewhere, and the dark-eyed gaze he turned in his wife's direction was hooded, shaded with hidden thoughts that she couldn't begin to understand.

'Why should anything be wrong? After all, we're both now going to get exactly what we want.'

What had put that cynical note into his voice, roughening it until it scraped her already over-sensitive nerves raw? But the truth was that ever since Keir had come back to her side at the start of the formal wedding lunch it had been clear that his mood had changed dramatically. The playful teasing that had so disturbed her had vanished, replaced instead by a darker, brooding distance.

'Well, you could at least act as if you were just the slightest bit pleased to be married to me,' Sienna hissed in the whisper necessitated by her determination not to be heard by her mother at her side and Keir's best man at his. 'If you continue to stare at your plate as if it was poisoned, and push the food around without tasting any of it, people will begin to wonder just what's wrong with you!'

Especially those who had just witnessed his Oscar-winning performance as the most lovelorn and devoted husband of the century.

'Right now you look more like the condemned man who can't even bring himself to eat his last meal…'

No, anger was the wrong approach entirely, drawing a disturbing response from him. Seeing the rejection that flared in his eyes, the way that one long-fingered hand clenched over the starched white damask of his napkin, Sienna hastily adjusted her tone and expression in the hope of appeasing him.

'It won't be long before this is all over,' she tried soothingly. 'There's just the traditional speeches and cutting the cake and then we can call it a day.'

Thankfully, she hadn't given in to the urgings of her friends and planned an evening party to round off the celebrations. She had been unable to square the idea with her already uncomfortable conscience, seeing it as taking hypocrisy way too far. And with Keir in this mood it would have been more like a wake than any sort of revelry.

'We'll soon be able to be on our own again.'

'And that will be so much better, will it?' Keir snapped coldly. 'Mr and Mrs Keir Alexander—oh, I'm sorry, I forgot. You want this marriage so little that you don't even think it's worth changing your name. So I see very little reason why you should be looking forward to our being alone…'

Sienna was astonished at how much his words stung. They were largely the truth, after all, so there was no reason for the sudden twist of pain she was experiencing.

With a sensation like the slow trickle of icy water creeping down her back, she found herself once more in the grip of the appalling unease of earlier that afternoon. It was as if some alien had moved in, taking over the shell of the person she had thought was Keir and replacing him with a total stranger.

But he was a stranger she was now legally tied to. For better for worse. For richer for poorer—in their case, definitely for richer, unless something went terribly wrong. Which it might do if she couldn't jolt him out of this black mood. Already interested eyes were turning their way, obviously made curious by their absorbed concentration on each other, the muttered conversation that was so clearly not made up of words of love.

There was just one way she knew to get through to him.

'Keir…' Deliberately she gentled her voice, making it softly sensual. 'Darling, don't be like this…'

She wasn't sure which startled him the most. The murmured endearment or the gentle hand she laid on his. But she couldn't be unaware of his reaction, seeing it in the sudden widening of his dark eyes. It was there under her fingertips too, in the tension that stiffened his muscles against her, the threat of rejection that he only just controlled in time. She knew how tempted he was to repulse her gesture in a response that would be totally inappropriate to the impression they were trying to create, and she knew just as surely exactly when he decided not to use it.

'I'm sorry.' It was a low, deep sigh. 'I'm just a bear with a sore head today.'

'A sore head!'

It was Sienna's mother who had caught the comment, her laughter-warmed tones lightening the atmosphere dramatically as she echoed his words, leaning forward to smile into Keir's dark, shuttered face.

'Would that be the result of rather too exuberant a stag night last night, son-in-law?' she asked teasingly. 'I would have thought you and your friends'd have more sense…'

'Now don't blame me!' James, the best man, joined in on a note of amused protest. 'Whatever Keir got up to last night, he did it on his own! And as for a stag night, all we had was a very sedate meal together at the beginning of the week, so you can't hold me responsible for the way he's feeling today. Unless you had some sort of debauched evening that you didn't invite me along to, you rogue,' he added, with a none too subtle dig of his elbow into Keir's ribs.

'Nothing of the sort,' his friend returned, switching on a grin that even came close to convincing Sienna, though she was well aware of how very far from genuine it actually was.

Along with the grin went a belated attempt to look affectionate, by turning his hand on the table top until his strong fingers enclosed hers completely, his grip warm and firm. The slow, deliberate movement of his thumb against the sensitivity of her palm dried her throat, the softly sensual circles he was drawing setting her heart thudding and heating her blood.

Keir's wicked, slanted glance in her direction told her that he knew exactly what he was doing. That he had turned her own weapon of the potent effect they had on each other back on her with devastating results.

'I'm afraid what was occupying me last night was business, pure and simple,' he confessed ruefully, his voice revealing nothing of the emotion that Sienna knew would shade hers if she tried to speak. 'A deal that needed finalising.'

'The night before your wedding!' James was obviously disbelieving. 'Keir, man, couldn't it have waited?'

'No way.'

The shake of his dark head that accompanied the flat statement was as firmly emphatic as the words.

'I wanted this particular matter behind me once and for all, so that I was free to concentrate on my bride. It's just that negotiations went on much longer than I had expected...'

Lucille had been as difficult as it was possible for her to be, damn her, Keir reflected grimly. She and her lawyer had held out for every penny she could get away with, and then some. There had been times when he had come close to giving up on the whole thing and walking out, but then, just when he had been about to declare that he had enough, that she could forget it, she had finally capitulated and signed on the dotted line.

'I didn't get to bed until well after midnight, and then I didn't sleep too well.'

'What was the problem?' Sienna inserted rather tartly, the sensual haze that had enclosed her evaporating with a rapidity that left her shaken and disturbingly on the edge of tears.

It was his comment about being free to concentrate on his bride that had changed her mood. She was only too well aware of the fact that it had been inserted solely for the benefit of their audience. It had no grounding at all in reality. In fact the real truth was that, crazily, she didn't even have the faintest idea what they were going to do once the wedding was over.

'Wedding nerves?'

'Something like that.'

'Oh, come on! That's the bride's prerogative, not the groom's!'

She couldn't believe that Keir—strong, independent, determined, cold-blooded, *heart-free* Keir Alexander—had lain awake worrying about the coming day. Refused to even consider that he might have felt as apprehensive as she had about the marriage ceremony and what they were getting themselves into.

Not Keir. He was the one who had been as cool as the proverbial cucumber all the way through this. Once she had convinced him it was the answer to both their problems, he had taken every single thing in his stride, handled each detail, every small hiccup, with the cool assurance that was so much a part of his nature.

'Are you saying that a man can't feel unsure and apprehensive on the night before his wedding—overawed by the prospect of what's ahead of him—the responsibility he's about to take on?'

'N-no…'

The look in his eyes disturbed her. They were darker than ever, shadowed by something she didn't understand. And now that she looked more closely she could see smudges of weariness underneath them, marks that she had never noticed before. The faint lines that fanned out from the corners of his eyes looked more pronounced too, as if etched there by strain and worry.

'Or are you claiming that if I'd rung you when I couldn't

sleep I'd have found you wide awake too, sharing the same sort of feelings?'

'Well—no, I wasn't.'

The truth was that, worn out by rushing around here there and everywhere for the past five weeks, she had fallen asleep as soon as her head had touched the pillow. Even the last minute butterflies in her stomach at the prospect of the day ahead had been overcome by the thought that tomorrow, finally, all her worries would be over.

'I didn't think so.'

Suddenly the thought that had crossed Sienna's mind a moment before came rushing back with a new and worrying force.

Once she had convinced him. Keir hadn't wanted this marriage. When she had first proposed the idea he had rejected it outright. It had only been when he'd made it a condition that they had a proper marriage, complete in every way, that he had been persuaded to agree to her proposal.

'Sienna!'

Her name in Keir's voice held a note of warning that dragged her back to the present. The best man was getting to his feet, ready to make his speech. Somehow Sienna found the self-control to appear to be listening. She turned her head in James's direction, focused her eyes on his face, and even, forewarned by the ripples of laughter from other parts of the room, managed to smile at the jokes he made.

But the truth was that she heard little of the witty address, and registered even less. Deep inside, her stomach was just a twisting mass of nerves, a knot of fear that made her stomach heave nauseatingly.

What had she done? She had actually asked this man to be her husband. To live with her, share her home, her life, her bed. For the next year, at least, she would have to make it appear that she and Keir were deeply in love. That they were no longer two individuals but that indefinable thing known as 'a couple'.

What had seemed so simple just a few days before now

seemed impossible, unendurable, fraught with pitfalls and traps to catch the unwary. The twelve months that had once appeared such a short space of time now stretched endlessly ahead, three hundred and sixty five days of it, and she had no idea how she was going to live through it.

Fear pounded inside her head, beating at her temples, so that she had to fight against the impulse to push her chair back and run from the room. She had chosen this path, knowing she had no alternative. Married to Keir she would inherit her father's money, and with it all the security and comfort it could bring. Without him she would be once more alone and desperate, with her mother totally dependent on her.

The speeches were over, the toasts completed. At last she was free from the obligation to stay in her seat. The feeling caused a rush of relief that brought her swiftly to her feet, unable to keep still any longer. She had no idea where she was going, thinking vaguely of heading for the huge French windows, now flung open in the late summer heat, of getting some much needed fresh air. Perhaps some deep, cooling breaths would calm her racing pulse, ease the pressure inside her head. But…

'Sienna…' Keir said abruptly, reaching for her. 'Wait…'

His grip on her arm felt like a steel manacle, imprisoning her. Panic flared afresh and, reacting purely instinctively, she tensed, pulling back, away from him, earning herself a dark, disapproving glare.

'What the…? Sienna, just what's got into you? People are looking!'

The savage undertone was somehow more disturbing than if he had actually raised his voice to express the anger he was clearly barely holding in check. The blaze in his eyes terrified her, and suddenly the ground no longer seemed steady beneath her, the thick red carpet shifting unnervingly under the soles of her white satin slippers.

'I won't go with you!' It was a desperate whisper. 'I can't!'

'Sienna, have you taken leave of your senses? Might I remind you that this is our wedding day?'

Remind her! As if she could forget!

'We have guests...people we should speak to.'

Speak! Sienna's tongue felt as if it was glued to the roof of her mouth, preventing her from forming a word. But with Keir's strong hand still clamped on her wrist, the other pressed firmly against the small of her back, she had no option but to follow him out into the room, somehow managing to acknowledge the greetings of the people they passed.

Her face seemed frozen into an expression of feigned happiness, the muscles around her mouth aching from smiling too many false smiles. All she wanted was to get away, be by herself, find peace and quiet in which to try to come to terms with what she'd done. But Keir was unrelenting in his determination that they should greet everyone. Ignoring her murmurs of protest, her obvious reluctance, he steered her from group to group, covering her awkwardness with the smooth ease of his own conversation.

'For God's sake!' he hissed in her ear. 'Now you're the one who looks like the condemned man! Smile, damn you! No one will believe you're madly in love with me if you look at me as if I was some deadly poisonous snake about to strike.'

'I *am* smiling,' Sienna retorted through clenched teeth. 'And as to looking as if I love you—I'd manage that much better if you didn't frogmarch me round the room as if I was either drunk or insane. I can manage to stand on my own two feet, you know. If you'd just let me go...'

'Be my guest!'

She was released so abruptly that she staggered awkwardly, afraid she might actually fall. Instinctively her hand went out to steady herself, and to her total surprise she found it taken by someone new. Soft fingers closed round hers, supporting her.

'Steady!' a female voice cautioned. 'You nearly took a tumble there.'

'Th-thank you.' With her balance restored, Sienna managed to turn to her rescuer with a smile more genuine than anything she had managed before.

'Not to worry,' she was assured. 'Those long skirts can be so very difficult to walk in when you're not used to them.'

'That's true!' The woman's perfume was rather cloying and overpowering, but Sienna struggled not to reveal her response to it. At last she felt something of her earlier panic receding, evaporating in the warmth of this new companion's smile. 'I'm sorry, I don't think. . .'

She didn't recognise the face. This must be someone Keir had invited. Someone she hadn't yet met.

'Keir, won't you introduce me…?'

But Keir stood at her side, stiff and withdrawn, his face appearing to have been carved out of the cold, immobile marble that formed the statues out on the terrace. Even his eyes were blanked off, revealing no emotion.

Why had this had to happen now? Keir asked himself furiously. If he had tried to think of the worst possible moment for Lucille to finally meet up with the woman he had married, then it would have been hard to imagine one that beat this. Sienna had already been behaving like a nervous thoroughbred, fearful of being handled for the first time, so he could just imagine how she was going to deal with this additional development.

The problem was that his new wife couldn't lie to save her life. She had come up with this ridiculous scheme of their pretend marriage, presenting it as the answer to all his problems as well as hers, but the truth was that she didn't know the half of it. She didn't know how appallingly Lucille had behaved—the sort of damage she was still capable of wreaking if given half a chance. And if his stepmother so much as suspected the true reasons behind this hastily arranged wedding, then she was more than likely to pounce on the information like some ecstatic predator. She would use it quite cold-bloodedly to her own advantage, especially if she could work on his own destruction at the same time.

'Keir…'

Just one word from the other woman's lips, but it had a dramatic effect on him. His head jerked round swiftly, his eyes narrowing to mere slits above his high, strong cheekbones.

'You want to be introduced? Well, fine. It had to be done some time, so I suppose now is as good an occasion as any. Sienna, darling, this is Lucille, my stepmother…' He spat the word out as if it left a foul taste in his mouth. 'Lucille, obviously this is Sienna, my wife.'

Lucille. Sienna couldn't believe what she was hearing. *This* was Lucille, the stepmother Keir so detested that he had finally agreed to their marriage solely because it offered him a way of getting rid of her, expelling her from his life once and for all? This was the monster who, like Medusa, had turned his heart to stone in the moment he had first seen her, and had never let a single redeeming chink of light into it since then.

But this woman was nothing like the one she had imagined. In her thoughts, influenced by Keir's own feelings, she had created a vicious harpy, cold-faced and cold-eyed, not this smiling, bright-eyed creature. And Lucille Alexander was so much smaller than she had anticipated, smaller and lovelier, with her peachy skin, green eyes and red-gold hair. But what rocked her back on her feet, threatening her balance again for a moment, was just how young Keir's stepmother was. She had anticipated some woman in her late forties, early fifties. This Lucille looked barely five or so years older than Keir himself.

'Sienna…' Lucille was holding out her hand. 'It's wonderful to meet you at last. I was beginning to wonder if I would ever get to see you at all. But now that I have I can quite understand why Keir wanted to keep you all to himself.'

'I doubt if you *understand* anything at all,' Keir put in with biting cynicism. 'And if I'd had my way you would never have been invited to the wedding. But Sienna wanted all my family here and, much as I hate to acknowledge it, you are family, if only by marriage…'

'Keir…!' Sienna put in reproachfully.

But Keir ignored her, his attention still fixed on Lucille.

'But, seeing as you are here, perhaps it's just as well. There's a small matter of business we can get out of the way. If you'll just follow me.'

Once again he clamped his hand over Sienna's arm, forcing her to go with him as he turned and marched towards the door. It was either that or be dragged inelegantly and embarrassingly in his wake. He didn't pause to look back and see if Lucille had followed them, apparently totally confident that she would do just that.

And it appeared that his confidence was not misplaced. When he finally came to a halt in the small private room the hotel had put aside for the bride and groom's use, Lucille was only seconds behind them. She was barely through the door before Keir kicked it shut, blocking off the noise and bustle of the reception.

'Now…'

Releasing Sienna abruptly, he reached into his inner jacket pocket, pulling out a long white envelope that he dropped onto the highly polished surface of a nearby table.

'This is what you're really interested in, dear stepmother. Oh, it's all right…' he added, seeing Lucille's curious glance in Sienna's direction. 'My wife and I have no secrets from each other. Quite the contrary. As a matter of fact, it's Sienna, not me, who's buying you out, at the price we agreed last night. Darling…'

It took Sienna the space of a couple of uneven heartbeats to realise that Keir was now speaking to her. And even when she had registered that fact she found herself staring at the fine silver pen he held out to her, unable to comprehend just what he had in mind.

'Sienna,' Keir urged softly. 'I need your signature. The document's all prepared. All you have to do is sign.'

And then it finally dawned on her just what he meant. Of course. This was what she had promised him in return for his agreement to go through with the wedding, his name on the marriage certificate.

But she hadn't expected him to hold her to her promise quite so soon. The ring was barely on her finger, the ink on that certificate barely dry, and already he was pushing her to complete her half of the bargain. She was quite unprepared for how much that hurt.

'Sienna,' Keir urged again, more forcefully this time. 'Sign it please.'

For a second or two Sienna was tempted to rebel. Let him wait for his money! He hadn't done anything to earn it!

But then Lucille spoke, and suddenly Sienna found that her mood had changed dramatically.

'So the little bride is bailing you out, is she Keir, darling? What a generous wedding present—I only hope she thinks you're worth it. But I'm sure you will be—in one important area of marriage at least.'

Her lascivious tone, the way her eyes gleamed, her pink tongue positively licking her lips, made it only too plain exactly what area she meant. Sienna could only stare, transfixed, unable to believe her eyes. It seemed as if the Lucille she had first met had vanished and another woman entirely had taken her place. This was the real stepmother, then, and she was beginning to understand just why Keir detested her so.

'You always did give great value there, didn't you, dearest? But I did wonder what had persuaded you to sign your freedom away like this...'

'I'm not signing anything away.'

Belatedly, it appeared that Keir had remembered the part he was supposed to be playing. Moving behind Sienna, he looped his arms around her waist, fastening his hands together under her breasts and pulling her back against him.

'On the contrary, I'm gaining everything I ever wanted. A beautiful wife, a new life with her, the prospect of a wonderful future...'

The sensual magic of his touch was working its spell all over again. Already Sienna could feel her body respond to the warmth of his, to the strength of his arms around her, the faint crisp scent of his cologne, so subtle and clean in contrast to the overwhelming reek of Lucille's perfume.

Instinctively she laid her head back against his shoulder, feeling his lips brush against her cheek as she did so. In this moment she could almost believe Keir had meant what he'd said. Could almost imagine that this was a real marriage, not the cold-blooded business deal Keir had just proved it to be.

'And naturally you're besotted with him.' Lucille turned a look of scorn on her. 'Well, I just hope you think you've got a good deal on this—that he's worth what you're paying him.'

Behind her, Sienna felt Keir's hard body stiffen in swift rejection. But his face showed no sign of what he was feeling and his hands continued their warm caresses over her arms and tracing the delicate lines of her neck.

'I'm not paying him,' she managed, her voice rather breathless as a result of the heightened, erratic beat of her heart. 'Nor am I bailing him out. What I'm doing is making our partnership a financial one as well as a personal one. An investment for our future.'

She must have sounded more convincing than she had hoped, because against her back she felt Keir's chest move in a silent, secret laugh of triumph.

For the first time Sienna felt a sense of unity with him. A feeling that they were both in this together, united against a common enemy. The sensation sent her spirits soaring, and impulsively she twisted in his grasp so that she could brush a kiss against the softness of his mouth.

'Give me the pen, darling, and show me where to sign. I

want the business side of things over with so that we can concentrate on more *personal* matters.'

In a haze of euphoria she signed her name with a flourish, folded up the document and thrust it back at Lucille, feeling a sense of exhilaration as the other woman took it and deposited it in her smart cream handbag.

'Well, I'll wish you every happiness together.' Lucille's tone implied exactly the opposite. 'You're obviously made for each other.'

It was as the door swung to behind her that Keir moved suddenly and unexpectedly. Sienna found herself gathered up into his arms and enclosed in a bear hug that drove all the breath from her body.

'Brilliant! You were quite perfect! You even had me convinced that you were crazy about me.'

'I did, didn't I?'

The warmth of his approval was doing strange things to her. The light in his eyes, the smile that curved the wide sensual mouth were as intoxicating as the fine champagne she had drunk earlier. She felt as if she was bathed in the warmth of the August sun outside, her skin glowing, her blood heating in response. It was a heady, thrilling sensation and she wanted more of it.

'And believe me, sweetheart, if you can convince my dear stepmother you can convince anyone. We might actually get away with this charade after all.'

Charade. Just one single word but it had an effect like the dash of icy water in her face. Sobering immediately, she felt herself come back down to earth with a sudden and very painful thud. His approval hadn't been for her, but for the performance he believed she had delivered.

Charade. Just for a second she had allowed herself to believe there was something else between them, some unity other than the one that linked them as partners in a scam to enable her to collect her inheritance. Something that would make the coming twelve months easier to live through. But she had only been fooling herself. Keir obviously wanted no such thing.

'So, now that's out of the way we can move on to the next stage...'

'The next stage?' Sienna's uncertainty showed in her voice. 'What next stage is that?'

'Really, Sienna, isn't it obvious?'

The look he turned on her was one of sardonic mockery, mixed with a strong dose of frank disbelief.

'We're married, darling. The wedding's over, the reception's coming to an end. What's the logical next move?'

'You don't mean...?' Sienna could only shake her head in disbelief. He couldn't mean what she thought.

'We do what everyone else does, sweetheart. We go on honeymoon.'

CHAPTER FOUR

HONEYMOON.

The word swung round and round inside Sienna's head as she lingered over a glass of wine on the terrace of the villa, enjoying the cool of the evening after the warmth of the day. Above her head, swallows swooped through the air in pursuit of midges, the swish of their wings the only sound in the silence that surrounded her.

'*We do what everyone else does, sweetheart. We go on honeymoon.*'

She had been frankly stunned by her own reaction to Keir's declaration. It had been the last thing she had expected. The nature of their arrangement was so businesslike and unemotional that she had never even dreamed there would be any place in it for of the conventional pleasures that were supposed to follow immediately after the celebration of a wedding.

So the realisation that they were actually to have a honeymoon had left her quite breathless and surprisingly excited. Somehow the thought of such a holiday had made her feel like a bride.

A *real* bride, she corrected when hard common sense had reminded her that she was actually Keir's bride, even if it was only a pretence at a love match.

'On honeymoon!' she exclaimed, looking up into Keir's dark face in wide-eyed surprise. 'But where...? What...?'

A strong finger laid across her lips silenced her effectively.

'That's my secret,' Keir told her with a grin. 'Isn't that what the groom's supposed to do? Organise everything and keep the destination a mystery until the last minute?'

It was more usual that the bride and groom chose the honeymoon together, poring over brochures and travel articles before deciding on some place they both wanted to visit, Sienna reflected, something of the euphoria that had lifted her spirits fading slightly. Of course there would be nothing like that for herself and Keir.

Discretion warned her that it would be best to make no comment about that. It would only spoil the new warmth that had developed between them. A warmth she very much needed. The last remnants of her earlier panic still lingered in her thoughts, clinging like sticky cobwebs to the corners of her mind, and she wanted desperately to drive them away.

'I didn't think we were having a honeymoon. If I'm honest, it never even crossed my mind.'

'A proper wedding, I said,' Keir reminded her. 'One with all the trimmings.'

'Yes, but this… I mean, can you afford it?'

Big mistake! *Bad* mistake. It was obvious that he didn't like what she'd said at all. The curve to his lips vanished at once, his face hardening ominously. The dark brown eyes took on a dangerous glint that warned her she had overstepped some invisible but firmly defined line that he had drawn around his private affairs.

Swinging away from her, he moved to stare broodingly out of the window into the spectacular garden beyond.

'I may have been forced to into needing a temporary injection of funds in order to meet Lucille's unreasonable demands, but I am still very far from penniless,' he snapped out, so sharply that Sienna found herself taking an involuntary step backwards, away from him. 'And even if I am only a temporary husband, hired for the period of our contract, I trust I know what my duties are—'

'Keir, don't! I didn't mean that the way it sounded!'

'Why not?' he flung over his shoulder at her. 'We both know you wouldn't have proposed marriage to me if you hadn't been desperate.'

'And you wouldn't have accepted if it hadn't suited your business plans!'

'Exactly.'

'You make it sound so sordid—so cold-blooded!'

With an abrupt, savage laugh Keir turned back to face her again, hands pushed deep into his trouser pockets, one black brow raised in taunting mockery.

'That's what business deals are, my lovely,' he told her harshly. 'Rational, hard-headed, and as cold-blooded as possible.'

If only that were really true, he reflected bitterly. If only he could have made *this* decision as coolly and unemotionally as he handled every other problem that he came up against in his working life.

But in this situation his natural control had totally deserted him. And the reasons for that were twofold. Both female. When it came to dealing with either Lucille or the woman now standing before him, the woman he had just made his wife, it seemed that common sense or rational thought went straight out of the window, leaving him uncharacteristically unsure of which way to turn.

As a result he had acted on the sort of impulse that he would have thought was totally alien to him, deciding to act before thinking things through to their logical conclusion. Only time would tell whether that decision would prove to be the best or the worst of his life.

'Why do you look so shocked?' he went on, seeing her big sea-coloured eyes darken in distress. 'You know I'm only speaking the truth. Those are the facts, so why should it worry you to hear them put into words?'

'I...' Sienna could only shake her head, unable to find an answer.

She couldn't deny the truth of what he had said. But it still disturbed her to have it stated so baldly, in the flat, emotionless voice Keir had used to deliver them.

'Conscience problems, sweetheart?' he questioned softly. 'Does it trouble you to discover that you might be every bit as cold-blooded and demanding as I am after all? That when you see something you really want you go for it with all the determination and ruthlessness you can muster up? And that in pursuit of your dream you can drive a harder bargain than anyone?'

His cynical words caught Sienna her on the raw, taking her breath away and making her want to lash out unthinkingly.

'If that was the case then you wouldn't be here right now!' she flashed at him. 'Believe me, if I could have what I *really want*, you wouldn't be the man with a wedding ring on his finger! And if I was to achieve a *dream*, then I would have married—'

'I know. Your precious Dean. The man whose shoes I couldn't possibly fill.'

The temperature in the small room suddenly seemed to have plummeted dramatically, making Sienna shiver convulsively in spite of the late August sun streaming in through the windows. She felt as if Keir's snarled words had been formed in freezing blocks of ice that had fallen brutally onto her delicate skin, chilling her where they landed.

With an effort she brought her dark head up, her face pale and her eyes clouded with remembered pain.

'Leave Dean out of this!'

'I would if I could,' Keir shot back, 'but you seem determined to keep flinging him in my face. I know that he's the one you really love, and that if you could have married him you would have done—but let me remind you of another truth, lady. One you obviously don't wish to face any more than all the rest.'

Keir's voice lowered suddenly, dropping to a low, dangerous whisper that was all the more menacing because of the softness of its tone.

'You haven't married Dean—you married me. As you just pointed out, *I* am the one with a wedding ring on my finger, not your precious lover-boy, who must be cursing his bad judgement in not staying around a little longer.'

'Judgement? Staying...?' Sienna frowned her confusion. 'I don't understand.'

'Oh, come now, darling, you understand only too well. You're not trying to claim that if dear Dean had stayed long enough to discover just how wealthy a young woman you are he wouldn't have had second thoughts about turning his back on you after all?'

Not for the first time, Sienna was thankful that she had never told anyone the full story of Dean's betrayal, but had kept the secret hidden away from prying eyes, especially Keir's.

'You think he would have married me for my money? You couldn't be more wrong.'

'I'm damn sure that he would never have been able to resist the lure of your inheritance, and he couldn't have turned down the opportunity of sharing it with you.'

'As you couldn't...' It was a low, despondent whisper.

'As I couldn't.' Keir confirmed brutally, his narrowed eyes dark and hard as jet, no trace of light showing in them. 'But there's one thing you must remember, my Sienna. One fact that differentiates me from the man you loved and lost and puts me here, with you, when he is who knows where, with God knows who. And that is that *you* proposed to *me*. You came to me with your idea of a marriage contract. *Me*. No one else. And we both know why you did that. Don't we?'

Sienna found it impossible to meet that cold, obsidian gaze. Nervously she dropped her eyes to stare at the floor, fixing them on the highly polished toes of Keir's handmade black shoes, planted firmly on the thick red carpet. But she couldn't block out the ruthless, inimical tones of that softly insistent voice as, seeing she was incapable of speech, Keir answered his question for himself.

'Of course we do. You wanted someone to act as your husband long enough to convince your newly discovered uncle that you were head over heels in love and to ensure that every penny of your inheritance was paid over. You needed someone who people would believe you might actually want to marry, someone who wouldn't disgrace you in public. But most of all you needed someone who you could bear to have in your bed…'

'No…'

It was a purely instinctual response, weak and thready, a protest against the grasping, avaricious picture he was painting with his words.

'Yes,' Keir corrected gently. 'Oh, yes, my darling. Any number of men would have married you for the price you were prepared to pay, but you asked me. It's easy enough to guess why.'

Transfixed, frozen into stillness, Sienna saw those shiny shoes come closer to her, Keir's footsteps silent on the soft, rich pile of the carpet. Unable to move away, she felt the soft brush of his skin against hers as his hand slid under her chin, his palm warm and hard as he impelled her face upwards. When she would have fought him, he simply applied a little more pressure, overcoming her resistance as if it had never been, until her rebellious blue-green eyes blazed into his, stubborn rejection of what he was about to say stamped into every line of her face.

'*This* is what you want from me…'

His gentleness was what took her by surprise, defusing her protest before it even had time to form. His kiss was the softest drift of his lips across her cheek, barely grazing the edge of her mouth in a way that had her moaning in involuntary disappointment.

Because even that featherlight touch was enough to spark off the hunger inside. Carefully calculated to awaken need, but not feed it, it was as unsatisfactory as it was enchanting. Involuntarily Sienna's eyes closed, her head turning in the direction of that tormenting mouth, seeking more, wanting a proper kiss, the sort that spoke of urgency and craving, communicating wordlessly the passion that flickered around them like the build up of static before a violent thunderstorm.

Close to her ear she felt Keir's warm breath, heard his softly triumphant laughter before she was rewarded with another kiss, only slightly more definite this time. His lips touched against hers, then danced away before she could respond, dropping brief, unfulfilling caresses on her cheek, her forehead, her closed eyelids and finally the dark silk of her hair.

'This is what burns between us, what neither of us can fight or deny. This…'

'Keir!'

The protest was torn from her, forming on her tongue before she had time to create any sort of coherent thought.

'What is it, sweetheart?' Amusement threaded through his voice, making it warm and teasing as once more those tormenting lips came close, then paused, only provocative inches away from her own. 'Tell me what you want and I'll give it to you.'

Determinedly keeping her eyes shut, Sienna still couldn't escape the scent of his skin, the faint sound of his breathing. It was more than she could bear, her self-inflicted blindness making every other sense excruciatingly sensitive to everything about him. She had never been more aware of the warmth of his body, the soft brush of his hair against her forehead as he leaned closer.

'Tell me!' he urged again, and the scent of his breath against her face was more than she could bear.

'Keir!'

In spite of herself, her eyes flew open, clashing with the dark intensity of his gaze so very close. Drowning in those chocolate-brown depths, she could no longer listen to the voice of common sense inside her head, heed its warnings, its reminders of the need for self-preservation.

'Kiss me, damn you! Kiss me properly before I go completely out of my mind.'

'Your wish is my command,' Keir muttered roughly, and

the next moment she was enclosed in iron-hard arms, hauled up against the wall of his chest and kissed with a thoroughness that made her head swim.

Without the strength of Keir's hands, clamped tight against the small of her back, she feared she might actually keel over, falling in a swooning heap on the carpet. She was incapable of supporting herself, clinging to the broad, straight shoulders under the fine cloth of his elegant jacket in a desperate attempt to keep herself upright.

Willingly she accepted the hard pressure of his lips, the teasing provocation of his tongue. With a sensual groan her mouth parted to welcome the intimate invasion, her body coming to life under the knowing caresses of his hands.

'Oh, Keir!' she sighed, snatching in a swift, much needed breath.

Her blood was a hot, bubbling stream that spread into every corner of her being, making every nerve, every cell spring into wild, yearning life. She felt that heat pounding against her skull, pulsing down her throat and along her spine, coiling around her heart and making her pelvis throb with molten need.

When his hard fingers curved over the swell of her breasts, their warmth searing into her sensitive flesh through the delicate lace that covered them, she writhed against him, her hunger spiralling as she felt the powerful evidence of his arousal. Beneath the soft silk that lined her dress, her sensitive nipples tightened, hardening in matching response. Simply knowing that he needed her as much as she wanted him made her thoughts spin off into a whirlwind of sensation.

Before I go out of my mind! Sienna thought, when finally the room stopped swinging round and she slowly resurfaced from the depths of sensuality into which she had fallen. She was there already, she admitted to herself. Totally crazed and incapable of rational thought where this man was concerned.

She didn't care if she was confirming everything he had

said about her reasons for marrying him. Couldn't care, because after all it was nothing more or less than the truth. In the first moment Keir Alexander had kissed her he had sparked off a conflagration of desire that was still blazing at white-hot intensity months later. She needed only a look, a word, a caress, or, as now, the touch of his lips against her skin, and she was lost, drowning in a sea of sensation with no wish at all to come up for air.

'Oh, lady, you drive me out of my mind,' Keir muttered against the soft skin of her arched throat. 'You make me forget everything I ever learned about civilised behaviour or gentlemanly conduct. When you're in my arms I feel as primitive as any caveman. I just want to drag you off to my bed, or push you against the wall, or down onto the floor…'

And she would let him, too, Sienna realised hazily. With the taste of his skin on her lips, the scent of his hair in her nostrils, the ragged sound of his breathing in her ears, she had completely forgotten who or where she was, and why. Her own need, urgent and demanding as his, would meet and match any move he made. Already, her impatient hands were under the elegant jacket, tugging avidly at the buttons on his shirt, anxious for the feel of his warm flesh underneath their seeking fingers.

'Sienna…'

Keir too needed more. His hands were under the fall of her veil, fumbling awkwardly with the tiny pearl buttons at the back of her dress, his actions made uncharacteristically clumsy with need.

'Sienna, you're mine—*mine*. You could never be with anyone else, never marry anyone else…'

Both so intent on each other, so absorbed in the elemental force that had them in their grip, they didn't hear the approaching footsteps or register that the door was slightly ajar until a voice they both recognised penetrated the burning mist that filled their thoughts.

'I've no idea where they are! But I've looked everywhere else, so perhaps they're down here.'

Mother!

Realisation hit Sienna in the same moment that Keir's head came up, wide dark eyes looking straight into her stunned aquamarine ones as they both froze into absolute stillness.

'Caroline!'

In instinctive reaction Keir jerked away from her as if he'd been stung, his hands coming up automatically to smooth down his clothing, fasten the buttons she had wrenched open. It was only now, seeing him a short distance away, that Sienna realised just what damage she had inflicted on his usually immaculate appearance. The sleek dark hair was wild and ruffled, his shirt pulled half out of the waistband of his trousers, his elegant tie totally askew.

Hot colour suffused her cheeks at the thought of what she had done, of how close they had come to being caught, the scene that might have met her mother's eyes.

'What's the problem, darling?' Keir had caught her response. 'Why are you so embarrassed.'

'You know why!' Sienna whispered, her hands twisting together in uncomfortable unease. 'If we hadn't heard... If she'd come in...'

'She'd have known that I was kissing you. So what?' Keir's shrug dismissed her concern as utterly unimportant.

'Kissing!' Sienna rolled her eyes in exasperation at the understatement. 'Keir, we were more than *kissing*...'

'And that's such a crime? Sweetheart, we're married! We're supposed to kiss—and more. In fact, I'm sure that's what your mother's expecting—why she's been careful to give us plenty of advance warning. Why do you think it's taking her so long to get down the corridor? I've never known Caroline bump into so many things, even if she does walk with a stick.'

Of course. Now that Sienna was able to think more clearly, she had to admit that her mother was making heavy weather of her progress towards them. And she was chattering at the top of her voice as she came.

But she would be here in a moment.

'Do I look all right?' she asked, suddenly painfully aware of the way Keir had restored his former elegant appearance and was looking totally composed and in control while she still felt flustered and distraught.

'You look fine.'

Keir turned a casually assessing glance on her, sliding from the top of her head down past her over-bright eyes and glowing cheeks and onto the square-cut neckline of her gown, where her struggle to regain control of her uneven breathing showed in the frantic way her breasts rose and fell.

'You look quite perfect—just as a newly married bride should be.'

Then, just as Sienna vented a deep sigh of relief, he added with a wicked grin.

'You look thoroughly kissed, sensually aroused, and bitterly frustrated at having your lovemaking session interrupted.'

'Oh, you…!'

Frantically she whirled round, hunting for a mirror to assess the damage, but too late. Behind her she heard Keir's soft laughter blending with the sound of her mother's voice calling her name.

'Sienna, darling! Keir?'

The door was pushed open and Caroline's thin form appeared in the doorway.

'Ah, there you are! I rather suspected as much. You wanted a little privacy—and who could blame you?' Her smile in Keir's direction was warmly conspiratorial. 'But your guests are getting a little restless, wondering where you are. I think it's time to cut the cake.'

'We were just coming.'

Sienna supposed she should be grateful for Keir's unruffled equanimity. She found herself unable to speak, to form any sort of coherent answer to her mother's questions. And when she turned to face the new arrival any chance of even thinking straight was driven from her mind. For behind Caroline, his bulky frame dwarfing her completely, stood Francis Nash, the man for whose benefit this whole pretence of a marriage had been staged. Her thoughts a blur, Sienna's eyes went automatically to Keir, instinctively seeking help.

He stepped into the breach at once, moving to her side with a smile that was every bit as loving and devoted as she could have wished as he slipped an arm around her waist and drew her close.

'We're just coming. I'm sorry if you thought us rude, slipping away like that, but I had something to tell Sienna, and I wanted to do it in private.'

'Of course! The honeymoon!'

Her mother's response so startled Sienna that at last she found her tongue was free to speak.

'You knew!'

'Of course she knew.' Keir's tone was softly indulgent. 'How else do you think I could arrange for your bags to be packed and your passport ready for us to leave at the end of the reception?'

The look he turned on Francis Nash was jokingly conspiratorial—men of the world together.

'I've arranged a surprise trip for my bride—one she knew nothing about. When I told her, she became rather emotional and—over-enthusiastic in her appreciation. I hope you don't feel neglected.'

'Er, not at all… I've been well entertained.' Francis returned, all the earlier suspicion Sienna had seen in him melting away in the warmth of Keir's deliberate charm assault.

'But now, my love, we have to go back to the reception. As your mother says, we've neglected our guests long enough.'

He was directing that charm at her now, the dark coffee-coloured eyes gazing deep into her stunned turquoise ones as if they were once more alone together. Hidden from the couple at the door by the bulk of his body, Sienna glared her feelings straight into his smiling face.

Rather emotional and over-enthusiastic indeed! How dared he?

'But first,' Keir went on sweetly, ignoring her silently communicated fury, 'I think perhaps a little repair work would be a good idea.'

Pulling an immaculate white handkerchief from his pocket, he tenderly wiped it around the curves of her mouth. It was only when he lifted it again and she could see that it had come away stained pink that Sienna realised how badly her lipstick had smudged in the heat of their shared passion just moments before.

The knowledge of what a mess she must have looked, and just how deliberately Keir had neglected to warn her of the fact, added fuel to her already burning anger. Struggling against the impulse to administer a smart, reproving kick to his ankle, she had to content herself with glaring even more fiercely at him as he considered his handiwork.

'There, now you look quite perfect.' Bending to brush a soft kiss against her temple, he whispered with laughter warming his voice, 'Don't glower so, darling. You'll ruin the good impression we've already made. Uncle Francis is totally convinced that we just can't keep our hands off each other.'

'And when I next get my hands on you…' Sienna hissed out of the corner of her mouth, only to find that her fury made him laugh even more.

'Promises, promises!' he returned, dropping another, casual kiss onto the tip of her nose. 'But I'm afraid you'll have to wait until we arrive at our honeymoon destination. Now, don't embarrass me in front of your family.'

Embarrass! This time Sienna did kick out at him, only to find that Keir had perfectly anticipated her reaction and, moving surprisingly quickly and neatly for such a big man, easily dodged out of reach. Caught off balance, she was forced to grab at his arm for support, knowing only too well that he was thoroughly enjoying her discomfiture.

Embarrass! The man didn't have an embarrassable bone

in his body, damn him! Her already ruffled mood was made all the worse by the fact that Keir had deliberately raised his voice on the last words, so as to make sure that her uncle and Caroline had heard his laughing comment too.

'It had better be somewhere I like!' she managed through clenched teeth.

'Oh, you'll love it!' her mother put in enthusiastically. 'Keir has been so thoughtful... He's chosen the *perfect* place.'

The warmly approving look she turned on her son-in-law sobered Sienna up in a rush. All anger seeped away from her, leaving her feeling unsettled and prey to disturbing thoughts.

This obvious affection that her mother had developed for Keir, the high esteem in which she so evidently held him, was a complication she couldn't possibly have anticipated when she had started out on this plan of a pretend marriage. But it had happened and there was nothing she could do about it. She could only wonder just how it would affect her mother when, in a year's time, she had to announce the uncontested divorce which was the way they had agreed this farce would end.

'Come on, sweetheart.' Keir's arm around her waist once more urged her out through the door. 'The sooner we get this cake cut, the sooner we can get out of here. It won't be long before we can be on that plane and alone together.'

Alone together. Sienna sat back in her chair, breathing in the warm night air. She and Keir were alone together now. Alone in this villa—this *Italian* villa.

Now she knew why her mother had been so excited, why Caroline had so obviously approved of Keir's choice of honeymoon destination.

Sienna herself hadn't had the faintest idea where she was going. Knowing she had no option but to do as he said, she had followed Keir blindly to the airport. Exhausted by the stresses of the day, the strain of having to pretend to everyone, to put on a show, even in front of her own mother, she had simply slumped in her seat, too tired, too drained even to ask or make any other effort to find out where they were heading. It had only been when their flight was called that she had had the first inkling of where she was to spend her honeymoon.

'Pisa!' she'd exclaimed, turning to stare at Keir in amazement. 'We're going to Italy!'

'That's right—Tuscany, to be precise. I thought you'd like to see the place where your mother met your father—the place you were named after. I've rented a villa just outside Siena.'

She had thought that things couldn't get any worse, but it seemed that fate had had this one final, ironic twist in store for her. Here, in the heart of the Tuscan countryside, where her father had met her mother, seduced her and abandoned her, leaving her pregnant, she was finally alone with the man she had to call her husband—at least for the next twelve months.

A faint movement, a flash of white, caught her vision at the corner of her eye. He was there. Keir had come out of the villa and was walking towards her. Slowly Sienna lifted her head and turned to face her husband. Here, where her mother had fallen hopelessly in love and been left alone and heartbroken, her own travesty of a marriage was to begin.

CHAPTER FIVE

HE HAD been watching her for some time.

In the shadow of the doorway, out of sight and unobserved, Keir had been standing silently, his long body leaning against the wall, just watching this woman who was now his wife.

God, but she was beautiful! With her long dark hair now loosed from the elaborate style that had confined it throughout the long day and tumbling down her back, her high cheekbones and full, softly sensual mouth, she made him think of the first time he had seen her. Then, he had anticipated that her eyes would be as dark as his own. It had only been when she'd turned, and he had seen with a sense of shock their soft, sea-washed colour, that he had fully appreciated the singular nature of her particular loveliness. And that appreciation had grown as he had come to know her.

As he had come to know her! Keir laughed silently, sardonically, at his own foolishness. He didn't know her at all. All he really knew was that instant, blazing physical attraction that had brought them together in the first place. An attraction that showed no sign of palling but which grew stronger with every day that passed.

Simply standing here, just looking at the delicate purity of her carved profile, the sensual curves of her body in the soft lilac dress, was enough to make him feel as he had been kicked hard in the gut, driving all the breath from his body and making him ache with need. But as to what was going on inside that exquisite head of hers—there he was truly groping in the dark.

That was why he had determined on this honeymoon. He

had known that she hadn't expected it, that she had believed they would simply go from their wedding to his home until the house she had inherited could be adapted for Caroline's use. And it had been that element of surprise that he had been aiming for, deliberately wrong-footing her.

He had brought her to Italy in the hope that here, on neutral ground, far away from home and the pressures that had driven her—driven both of them—to start out on this counterfeit marriage, he would finally begin to find out just what made this wife of his tick.

But some slight sound he hadn't been aware of making, a movement he hadn't controlled, had alerted her to his presence. Her head had turned; he had no alternative but to join her.

'What were you doing, lurking there in the shadows?'

'I wasn't lurking,' Keir returned cagily. 'I was simply watching you.'

'Watching me?' It was clearly not what she had expected. 'Why?'

'Because I like looking at you. Why not? Can't a man look at his wife?'

Sienna reached for the wine bottle on the table in front of her, her movements edgy and uneven, like her voice.

'We're not the normal sort of man and wife. Some wine?'

'Thanks…'

He took the glass with deliberate slowness, letting his fingers linger on hers for a couple of seconds, meeting her wary gaze head-on.

'So it's not normal for a man to find his wife beautiful?' he asked quietly, lifting his drink to his lips.

Sienna had been about to sip from her own glass, but now she set it down with a distinct tremor that had her hastily reaching to steady it before it fell over, spilling its contents onto the stone flags.

'Of course that's normal! I simply meant that you don't have to put on the big romantic act just because we're on honeymoon. After all, we both know it isn't real.'

'Who said it was just an act? I do think you're beautiful and I want you to know it! And as for romance—we're in Italy. One of the most romantic countries in the world—'

'Not for my mother,' Sienna cut in sharply. 'I doubt if she thinks of her time here in that way. I mean, all it led to was betrayal and heartbreak.'

'You couldn't be more wrong.'

'Oh, so now you know my mother better than I do?'

'Have you talked to her about it?' Keir set his glass down with rather more care than she had used earlier. 'Really talked? I think you'll find that her memories are much happier than you imagine. They're of a time was she was in love and loved in return…'

Sienna's cynical snort of disbelief made it only too plain what she thought about that.

'Okay—she *thought* she was loved. And even though it ended unhappily she doesn't regret having had that experience.'

'"Better to have loved and lost than never to have loved at all"?' Sienna quoted satirically.

'Exactly.'

'You'll have to forgive me if I disagree.'

'You don't believe that having known Dean was worth it?' Keir enquired, with a deceptive mildness that Sienna privately felt hid a very different frame of mind. 'That having known love, even if only once, was—'

'I don't think that anything about Dean was worth it!' Sienna snapped, anxious to cut off that line of questioning once and for all. 'In fact, I truly wish I had never, ever met him!'

She didn't like the look he gave her, or the way one dark straight brow lifted slightly, questioning the truth of her overly vehement declaration.

'And I don't want to talk about him or anything to do with him. Does my mother really have happy memories of Siena?' she asked, because she couldn't help herself.

Keir's dark head nodded slowly as he swallowed another mouthful of wine.

'One of the most memorable times of her life, she told me. She also said that it was impossible to have anything but good thoughts about a time and a relationship that resulted in her having you.'

'You *have* talked, haven't you?' The words came out jerkily, made that way by the unpleasant sensation of unease that was pricking at her, rather like mental pins and needles.

'Your mother is very easy to talk to, and our conversations are always wide-ranging and stimulating. I like Caroline, and I think she likes me.'

'Oh…'

Hastily Sienna reached for her glass again, burying her nose in it so that the dark curtains of her hair fell down on either side of her face, hiding her expression from him.

It was impossible not to think of the way her mother had looked at Keir as they'd left the wedding reception. The warm, approving smiles, the obviously genuine emotion in the hug she had given him as they'd said goodbye. A hug Keir had been only too keen to return, she now recalled. All her anxieties about Caroline's affection for her new son-in-law and the potential problems that might result from that came rushing back in a distressing flood, making her shift uneasily in her seat.

'I wish you wouldn't.'

'Wouldn't what? Talk to your mother? Sienna, I am her son-in-law.'

'Temporary son-in-law. What—?'

She looked up in shock as Keir's glass in turn was slammed down on the table top.

'Well it's true!' she protested sharply.

'*You* know it's true. *I* know it's true.'

The statement was cold and clipped, and Keir's eyes, gleaming disturbingly in the moonlight, were hard, distant and unapproachable.

'But I thought the whole idea was that *no one else* should

know—that everyone should believe our marriage was the genuine thing. It's going to look pretty damn strange, not to mention unconvincing, if I don't even try to make an effort to get on with your mother, especially if she's going to live with us.'

Put like that, there was no denying how right he was. The very reasonableness of his tone made her feel all sorts of a fool for even having raised the subject.

'It's just that I don't want her hurt. She's had enough pain in her life, and now that she's ill I don't want her to put up with any more.'

'I can understand your concern, but really there's no need for it.'

Leaning forward, Keir took hold of her hand where it lay on the table, curling his warm, strong fingers round it.

'Believe me, I would never hurt your mother, Sienna. You must know that.'

'I—I know…'

Sienna wanted to believe that the unsteadiness of her reply was the result of his touch. That the simple contact had sparked off the usual mind-blowing physical response that she experienced with him. But to her consternation she found that the truth was much more complicated.

I would never hurt your mother. She had no hesitation in believing that. But would he offer the same assurance for Sienna herself? Would he be able to say, with the same conviction, I will never hurt *you*?

And the fact that she was even considering the problem was the most disturbing part of it. She would have said that nothing Keir could do could ever hurt her. After all, wasn't that why she had chosen him? Because in their relationship there were no unwanted complications, like emotional involvement of the sort that, after Dean, she was determined to avoid like the plague? So how could anything he did affect her badly enough to cause pain?

'Why the big sigh?'

To her horror she had betrayed the way she was feeling,

and Keir had caught it. Immediately she jumped onto the defensive, too shocked by her unexpected thoughts to try to explain them even to herself.

'I was just thinking of my mother, and—Andrew Nash. I still can't think of him as my father.'

'That's hardly surprising. After all, you never even saw him. And a father is so much more than someone who plays a physical part in your conception. Andrew Nash forfeited his right to that title when he walked out on your mother twenty-six years ago. A belated bequest in his will doesn't alter anything. Did I make a mistake, Sienna?'

'A mistake?'

Sienna frowned her confusion as much at his change of tone as at the question itself. Keir had lowered his voice until it was a softly husky whisper, a sound that brushed over the ends of her nerves in a way that made her shiver in disturbed response.

'In bringing you here? Did I make the wrong decision when I chose Italy for our honeymoon? Would you have preferred France, or perhaps somewhere exotic—a beach and palm trees?'

'No!' Sienna hastened to reassure him, amazed to find that he sounded as if it actually mattered to him. 'No, it wasn't a mistake. Mum's talked about Tuscany so much, and I've always wanted to see it for myself.'

Feeling suddenly disturbed and restless, she got to her feet, moving to lean against the stone wall that edged the terrace, staring out into the countryside, now completely dark except for a few scattered lights.

'Which way is Siena? North or south?'

'South—that way…'

Keir came to stand beside her, pointing away to their right.

'And Florence is in the opposite direction, back on the road we drove along on our way here from Pisa.'

'I can't wait to see the countryside in the daylight.

Everyone I know who's been here tells me it's spectacularly beautiful.'

'It is.'

Keir's response was distracted. This was like making polite conversation with a stranger, he thought uncomfortably. They were pussyfooting around each other in a way that only made his already unsettled mood worse. This was not at all how he had expected to feel on his wedding night.

What *had* he expected? When his mind threw the question at him he had no idea how to answer it. If the truth was told, he was working completely in the dark, unable to see what move to make next.

But one thing he *had* anticipated. He had thought that by now he would be feeling a great sense of freedom. That with Lucille off his back, the debt of honour paid to his father, he would be experiencing a sort of release from the problems that had beset him that would be close to euphoria.

Instead, he felt low and flat, in a way that, combined with the restless unease that had assailed him ever since he had woken, made him as jittery as a cat on a hot roof. Instead of experiencing a sense of liberty, his mood was dark and oppressive, as if he had exchanged one form of obligation for another. And right now he wasn't at all sure that he wouldn't prefer the uncomplicated financial contract with Lucille to the one that he was subsequently tied to.

'You've been here before?'

'A couple of times. The last holiday we had as a family was in Tuscany. That was the year before my mother died.'

Perhaps it was because of the gathering darkness, but the bleakness of his tone sounded disturbingly clear, making Sienna wince inwardly.

'That was when you were how old?'

'Nineteen. I'd just finished my first year at university, and I wasn't at all keen on the idea of going away with my parents. I took a lot of persuading, but I'll always be grateful that I went along in the end. Six months later, she discovered she had leukaemia. Four months after that, she was dead.'

'Oh, Keir…' It was the first time he had ever talked about his mother's tragically early death, and Sienna found that she was deeply touched that he had opened up in this way. 'I'm so sorry.'

Instinctively her hand went out to cover his strong fingers where they lay on the stone parapet. This would partly explain the warmth of his relationship with her mother. Having lost his own parent so early, he must feel the need to revive something of the relationship they had shared with Caroline.

And perhaps it also went some way towards clarifying why he had agreed to her proposal in the first place. He would know how it felt to have a sick mother. Know the feeling that you would do anything at all to make her life easier.

'And how long was it before your father married again?'

'Four years.' His mood had obviously darkened. Asking about Lucille had been a mistake.

But Sienna's curiosity got the better of her.

'She's much younger than I ever expected.'

'Barely forty.' Keir nodded. 'Only seven years older than me.'

Something bleak and disturbing shaded his voice, sending a shiver down Sienna's spine in spite of the warmth of the evening,

'She—'

'Leave her out of this, Sienna,' Keir commanded. 'I don't want my stepmother intruding on my wedding night.'

'*Your* wedding night!'

In spite of herself, Sienna took a small step backwards, unable to control her instinctive response. In her excitement at actually being in Italy she had managed to forget why they were there. She had been able to push from her mind all thought of what was ahead of her, but that possessive 'my wedding night' had brought it rushing back in a way that made her heart jerk in nervous reaction.

'Yes, of course.' To her horror she realised that he had caught the whisper she hadn't been able to hold back, the sudden sharpening of his tone making her mouth dry nervously. 'What is it, Sienna? You're not planning to back out of our agreement, are you?'

'N-no. It's just…'

She couldn't complete the sentence, her throat closing up around the words. It was one thing to agree to the conditions he had imposed in the heat of desperation, when the date of the wedding had still been in the future and the idea of actually going to bed with him had only been just that—an idea, not fully founded in reality. It was quite another to accept that she had used up all her waiting time, that Keir had called in his account, and that right here and now was when she had to start paying.

'Hey!' Keir's voice was surprisingly soft. 'Don't look so panic-stricken. I won't hurt you.'

'I—I know!'

Sienna cursed the quaver in her voice. She had told herself she could do this; convinced herself that, when it came to it, the blazing physical response she felt whenever he touched her would burn away all her fear, all restraint.

But that was when she had pictured Keir literally sweeping her off her feet. When she had imagined him gathering her close and kissing her stupid, driving all thoughts from her mind except the fact that he was a man and she was a woman, and that the need that had brought them together was as old and as elemental as time.

But Keir was making no move to do anything of the sort. Instead of taking her in his arms, he had actually moved a couple of steps backwards, away from her. Instead of the blazing passion she had anticipated, hoped for, there was a cool, unnerving distance, a perturbingly detached sense of circumspection about him. Those dark eyes narrowed thoughtfully, subjecting her to an emotionless scrutiny that made her shift uneasily from one foot to another.

'Do you think I'll force you, is that it? Damn it, Sienna,

don't you know me better than that? I've never bullied a woman into my bed, and I don't intend to start now.'

Perhaps it would be easier if he did, Sienna found herself thinking weakly. At least that would heat the blood that seemed to have frozen in her veins, break through the ice that surrounded her like sheets of plate glass.

She could see Keir's strongly carved face, the softness of his hair stirred by a faint breeze. She could hear his words, blurred slightly by the pounding of her pulse inside her head. But she couldn't make herself move to bridge that gap between them.

'Sienna!'

Her name hissed in between clenched teeth in a sound so expressive of impatience and obdurate demand that she shivered involuntarily. But almost immediately his mood changed again.

'Oh, hell! Look, Sienna, it's been a long day. You're tired. I want you in my bed, yes, but I want you willing. We have twelve months—that's more than enough time.'

'Enough time to take what you want and tire of me?' Sienna couldn't catch the impetuous, unthinking words back, even though she wished she'd never spoken as she saw his proud head go back, brown eyes flashing in bitter anger.

'That really rather depends on you,' he flung back. 'But I for one am not prepared to rush…'

Shaking his head, he raked both hands through the darkness of his hair.

'It's been a stressful day. If you want a little time—a breathing space—I understand. This villa has four bedrooms. If you'd rather sleep alone for tonight, then choose whichever one you want.'

'What?'

Sienna knew she was gaping at him, her confusion and disbelief clear on her face. Did he mean…? Could he mean…?

A tiny, craven part of her mind wanted to grasp at the

opportunity he offered. To take the chance to sleep alone for one last night. But, even as she let the thought slide into her mind, another, more worrying one replaced it.

For tonight, Keir had said, with a deliberate emphasis that left her in no doubt that one night's grace was all she was going to get. Tonight he might be feeling indulgent, generous to a fault because he'd got what he wanted, but tomorrow, and every other night that followed would be a very different matter.

After the proper wedding we have a real marriage. Those had been Keir's terms. There was no way he was going to free her from their arrangement, not without completely retracting what he had promised.

To delay would only make matters worse. The apprehension she felt now would never diminish, only grow worse with each second that passed.

And so she drew herself up, plastered on a smile that she hoped looked more convincing than it felt.

'Don't be silly, Keir!' Her lips felt stiff and wooden, forming the words with difficulty. 'We can't sleep alone. We're married! On honeymoon.'

'But as you've already pointed out, this isn't exactly the normal sort of honeymoon.'

Dark eyes probed hers, seeming to reach deep into her very soul, to try to read what was there. Sienna was sure that he must be able to see the way her heart seemed to be turning somersaults inside her chest, making her breath come in rapid, uneven gasps.

'Though I have to admit I'm forced to wonder just what constitutes ''normal'' under these circumstances.'

Sienna tried to speak, found it impossible, and ran a nervous tongue over her parched lips in order to moisten them.

'I'm sure that any husband would expect to—to sleep with his wife on the first night of their married life. And y-you more than most.'

'And why me more than most, my lovely Sienna?'

His tone had changed, darkened, the emphasis on that 'why me' ominously dangerous.

'We had a bargain. You'll want to claim what you're owed.'

In the gathering shadows it was almost impossible to read his expression clearly. But she couldn't be unaware of the black scowl that distorted his features, menacing as a thundercloud gathering on the horizon.

'You make it sound as if I'm collecting on a bad debt. And besides, you've already given me most of what you promised, so I can afford to be generous.'

Most of what you promised! The words slashed at her like a blunt knife, leaving a raw, bleeding wound. She could be in no doubt as to what he had meant.

He had wanted the money she had promised him to pay off his stepmother, and she had already guaranteed it. Hadn't he had the document waiting, ready to be signed just as soon as their marriage vows had been spoken?

Did she need any further evidence of just how little she meant to him? A real marriage, indeed! He meant no such thing! What he wanted was the best deal he could get.

His coldly calculating mind had assessed what she had offered him, weighed it against what she was asking in return, and decided he could agree to her terms. There was no emotion involved, not even the passion she had been foolish enough to assume. His financial acumen had recognised a good deal when it was offered, and the sexual opportunist in him had added the urge to gain some easy physical pleasure from the arrangement; that was all.

Of course he could afford to be generous! He had her right where he wanted her—and that was very much in second place to his damn business!

The realisation was like a rush of adrenaline in her mind, surprising her by the sense of freedom it brought. If Keir's emotions were so totally uninvolved in their arrangement, then surely she could match him step by step. She could use him as he planned to use her, taking the sexual pleasure their union could provide and giving nothing more.

And at the end of the year she would walk away, as heart free as he was.

'Yes, you have been generous.' Even in her own ears, her voice sounded cold and stilted, bringing the temperature around them down by several calculated degrees. 'After all, you have signed away your freedom in order to help me.'

She knew by the way that the long body before her moved restlessly that he had caught her reference to Lucille's comment at their wedding. Heard it and hadn't liked it at all.

'But we had an agreement, Keir, and I intend to fulfil my part of that deal. That way, no one can ever claim they were short-changed.'

'Oh, I would never claim that, sweetheart.' Keir's tone matched hers ice for ice, making every tiny hair on her skin lift in response. 'So far you've been scrupulous in complying with the letter of our contract.'

There was a distinct bite of acid on the last words that Sienna struggled to ignore.

'And I intend to deliver what I promised.'

'In that case…'

Hard face unsmiling, brown eyes totally lacking in warmth, Keir held out his hand to her.

'Shall we go upstairs?'

CHAPTER SIX

IT TOOK every ounce of courage that Sienna possessed to put her hand into his. The feel of his hard fingers closing around hers made her think of a trap snapping shut, and it was all that she could do not to start nervously, snatching it away from him as if she had been burned.

Without a word he led her into the house and upstairs, to the large, oak-beamed, simply furnished room which, on their arrival, he had declared would be where they would sleep for the duration of their stay. The shutters were fastened over the windows, making the room shadowy and dark, and the cool of the air-conditioning was almost shocking after the warmth of the evening outside. Within seconds, Sienna's skin felt chilled and clammy, and she had to struggle not to shiver openly. To do so would be to risk Keir thinking that her response was one of fear, and she was determined to hide her inner misgivings from him.

The maid had long ago unpacked their belongings and put them away. But some appallingly sensitive instinct, or, more likely, some instruction from Keir himself, had warned her that this was more than a simple holiday, but was supposed to be a honeymoon. And so, as Sienna followed Keir through the door, the first thing that caught her eye was the careful drape of her white silk nightdress, long-skirted, with a delicate lace bodice and shoestring straps, over the pillows on one side of the bed.

The *double* bed, she registered, her heart skipping a painful beat, A bed that, with its soft blue cotton cover, seemed to totally dominate the whole room, making it impossible to look anywhere else. Just the sight of it made her head spin, her legs weaken beneath her, and unthinkingly she tightened her grip on the strength of Keir's hand.

'Steady, my lovely.' His low voice gentled her as if she was some nervous, thoroughbred mare he feared might bolt.

The thought of doing just that had flashed into her mind. Into it, and straight out again, driven away by a mixture of careful rationalisation and fierce, determined pride.

Running away would do no good at all. It would only delay the inevitable. And the thought of the humiliation of being pursued, caught, and dragged back to this room again was more than she could bear. She had made her bed, Sienna thought, gritting her teeth against an impulse to near-hysterical laughter. Made it and must now resign herself to lying in it, with Keir at her side.

'There's no need to be nervous. We can take this as slowly as you'd like. We have all the time in the world.'

Sienna's free hand, clenched into a tight fist, went to her mouth, crushing back the whimper of distress that almost escaped her. How could she tell him that time was not what she needed? That the last thing she wanted was for this to be slow?

Time would give her too much opportunity to think. To register what was happening to her and know that there was no way out. Time would leave her in no doubt at all that this was a business deal and nothing more, offering her no comforting emotions like love or passion to smooth away the rough edges, soften the hard truth of this cold-blooded seduction.

What she needed was the whirlwind of sensation that had assailed her whenever Keir had kissed her in the past. The heated tornado of need that had taken possession of her mind, leaving her incapable of thought, able only to feel, to hunger, to *yearn*. Blinded by that storm of emotion, she could get through this. Any other way and it might destroy her.

But Keir still seemed strangely reluctant to touch her.

Instead, he led her into the middle of the room, dropping her hand and turning to face her.

'Perhaps you'd like a while to yourself? Time to…' the dark-eyed, sombre gaze went to the nightdress on the bed and then to the door of the adjoining *en suite* bathroom '…refresh yourself. Get ready…'

Too numb to speak, Sienna could only nod silently. But as he made a move to walk away the panic that had been twisting in her stomach rose to the surface, telling her in no uncertain terms that this was the last thing she wanted.

'No!'

It was a choked cry, impossible to hold back, and, hearing it, Keir froze before swinging round sharply.

'No?'

'No, I don't want to be left alone like some virginal Victorian bride, while my groom goes downstairs for one last drink, leaving me to get modestly into bed and lie there, waiting. I don't want to bathe, brush my hair, perfume my skin, so that my husband will enjoy taking his conjugal rights—taking me—making me his. That might be appropriate if…'

The words died on her lips, shrivelled into nothing by the fierce blaze in his eyes, the smouldering fury that was so near to the surface he was obviously having to exert all his strength simply to rein it in.

'If this was a real marriage?' he finished for her, with a clipped acidity that made her wince away in misery. 'And you have been so determined to impress on me that it's not. But it *will be* a real marriage, my sweet Sienna, at least for the period arranged by our contract. A real marriage or no marriage—the choice is yours. Are you saying that you want this marriage annulled, revealed as the farce that it is?'

Wide and clouded, Sienna's sea-coloured eyes went to the silk nightdress on the bed. The nightdress that her mother had bought for her, her thin face alight with happiness as she presented it to her daughter as part of her trousseau, telling her to wear it on her wedding night in order to be a beautiful bride for her wonderful husband.

If she called a halt now, how could she face her mother again? And not just because of the inheritance that would then no longer be hers. How could she disillusion Caroline, reveal to her that the wonderful, fairy tale, happy-ever-after marriage that she had believed in was nothing but an illusion, a fantasy dreamed up quite cold-bloodedly for purely materialistic reasons? Not that those reasons could be described as *pure*, she reflected miserably.

'N-no…' she said hesitantly. 'That's not what I want.'

'Then what *do* you want? Come on, Sienna,' Keir urged huskily. 'You've been so determined to let me know what you *don't* want. Isn't it time you started coming clean about what you *do*?'

'I—I…'

His eyes were so deep and dark that she couldn't look away, finding her gaze instead drawn and held, transfixed as if she had been turned to stone.

This must be how it felt to be hypnotised, she thought hazily. This feeling that she had no will of her own, but must wait, quiescent and resigned, like a discarded marionette, until the man before her pulled the strings or issued a command that would tell her what to do.

'Say it,' Keir said now, his whisper shivering through the still air. 'Tell me what you want and it can be yours.'

And suddenly it was so easy. Suddenly she knew what she wanted, as if there was nothing else in the world. There was only the hushed silence of the night, and this room, this man and herself, and a communion between them that was as old and as primitive as time.

It was there in the depths of his black, enlarged pupils, in the streak of hectic colour high on the wide cheekbones. It echoed through every uneven breath and in the rapid, jerky patter of her own heart. And in that moment she knew that she had stopped running and that everything she wanted was right here, right now, in this room and nowhere else.

'I want you to kiss me.' Her voice croaked slightly, but it surprised her with the strength and conviction she managed. But still she had to repeat herself, so there could be no mistake. 'Keir, I want you to kiss me…'

'I thought you'd never ask!'

He moved so quickly that she barely saw him. All she knew was that suddenly he was there, with her, enfolding her, surrounding her with the warmth and strength of his body. With one arm at her waist, another at her shoulders, he held her tight up against him, her head bent back while his mouth plundered hers with a fierce hunger that held all the wild heat of the fires burning deep inside him.

And it was just as she had imagined. Just as she had hoped. There was no room for thought, only for feeling. Nothing in her mind but sensation. Nothing in her heart but a flame that matched and outstripped the blaze in his. Nothing in her body but the tempestuous, unbridled hunger that made her shudder with need, her moan a feral, uncontrollable sound expressive of a hunger so deep she had never been fully aware of its existence.

But she knew of it now. It was as if the floodgates inside her had been flung open and she was powerless against the force of the torrent that stormed through, sweeping everything else before it.

'I want you to kiss me,' she muttered again, her voice shaking with a sort of desperation. 'I want you to hold me, and touch me…'

She had no sense at all of having formed the whispered litany of need, only that it tumbled from her lips like a prayer. And that Keir obeyed every request without protest or hesitation.

'I want you to caress me, stroke my skin, make me want you, make me need you.'

'You've got it, darling…' Keir's response was a rough, thickened whisper, his voice muffled against the delicate skin of her throat where his lips blazed a burning trail down towards the racing pulse at the base of her neck. 'Anything you want. Everything you want.'

His hands were at the back of her neck, where the zip fastening of her lilac dress gave him far less trouble than the buttons on her wedding dress had hours earlier. With a faint rustle the delicate material slid down from her shoulders, paused for a moment before she dropped her arms to free it, then slithered all the length of her body to pool in a crumpled heap on the floor at her feet.

This time, Sienna's shiver was one of excitement and anticipation. All the nervousness of moments before had vanished, burned up in the heat that raged through every vein, every nerve-ending, making her skin glow as if it was bathed in the heat of the Tuscan sun and not the cool, shimmering gleam of moonlight.

Her eyes were closed, her body trembling under the onslaught of the sensations that ripped through her. Keir's touch now seemed to be everywhere. On her face, on her arms, smoothing over the rounded curves of her shoulders, sliding down to encircle and cup the warm weight of her breasts.

Against the hard heat of his hands, her sensitised nipples peaked, pressing an urgent message of need into his palms. And lower down, at the core of her most feminine being, the throbbing sensation that started up was like a burning electrical current, sending shockwaves radiating out into every other part of her.

'I want you to make me yours, make me forget about everything else, anything else. I want you to make this into the experience I know it can be. I want you to make it—make it real…'

Make it real! The words reverberated inside Keir's head as her voice choked off on a sigh of delight at some particularly pleasurable touch of his strong fingers. *Make it real!* Dear God, if she only knew!

With his rational mind scrambled by the beating, insistent clamour of every one of his senses, totally at the mercy of the hunger that throbbed inside him, tormenting the most sensitive parts of his anatomy, he almost told her. He almost opened his mouth and blurted out the truth, realising only at the very last moment that to do so would be to ruin everything. Gritting his teeth with the effort, he swallowed down the betraying words.

'Make it real, sweetheart?' he muttered, his tone raw and uneven. 'I can't promise you that. But I can promise you that what we have together will be very special. I promise you a honeymoon you'll never forget.'

'Show me.' It was part request, part command, part sigh of hunger. 'Show me what you—'

The words were crushed back down her throat as once more his mouth fastened on hers, lips fusing hungrily together. Somehow he had shrugged out of the polo shirt he wore, the heated silk of his skin smooth under her hands as she writhed against him in pleasurable abandon. Each second piled sensation on sensation, opening her mouth to him, adding that bit more fuel to the fires of passion they had built between them.

With confident ease he stripped off the wisps of silk that were all she wore, tossing them aside so that they floated like drifts of gossamer onto the polished wood of the floor. Against the yearning sensitivity of her now naked breasts the faint roughness of his body hair was a stinging delight, making her gasp her response into his demanding mouth. She felt the burning power of his arousal pressing against her, and instinctively opened her thighs so that she could accept him into the cradle of her hips.

With a muttered curse Keir gathered her up into his arms, lifting her completely off her feet and carrying her to the bed, where he flung back the covers with a violent gesture, depositing her none too gently on the soft linen sheets. Pausing only to discard his own remaining clothing, he came down beside her, his long, muscular body dark against the pastel bedding, his skin hot to her touch.

'I knew it would be like this,' he muttered thickly. 'Knew

it from the moment I kissed you. You're so responsive to me, and that just blows me away. I can't think straight…'

Watching her intently, he dropped a swift kiss on one pink nipple, then slowly encircled it with his tongue, laughing deep in his throat as she squirmed in breathless, whimpering excitement.

'And neither can you. Do you know what it does to me to see you out of control like this?'

'I—I can see what it does. . .' Sienna managed on a shaken laugh, turquoise eyes widening as she took in the full impact of his powerful nakedness, the potent force of his masculinity. 'How could I be unaware…?'

Her fingers trembling slightly, she reached out to touch him, laughing again, but this time on a note of triumph as his powerful body convulsed at her touch, the shudders of delight that shook him giving her an overwhelming sense of power. How was it possible that this strong, cold-blooded man could be at her mercy like this? How could she have brought him to this state, where each breath rasped into his lungs so painfully, where his eyes were and glazed with uncontrollable desire?

'You witch!' he reproved softly. 'Do that again and I won't be answerable for the consequences.'

'Perhaps the consequences are exactly what I'm after,' Sienna teased, her turquoise eyes gleaming provocatively from behind the silken fall of her long dark hair. 'Perhaps I want—'

'I know *exactly* what you want,' Keir broke in on her. 'You want to know how you make me feel. You want to experience something of the same. Well, when you touch me here…'

Briefly he held her hand against the slick, hard heat of him, then pushed her back against the softness of the pillows, supporting himself on his elbows on either side of her slender frame.

'It feels like this…'

His dark, arrogant head bent to take her right nipple into

his mouth, suckling hard. The warm breath of his laughter feathered over her skin as, unable to control her response, she reared up against him, shifting from side to side as a hot current of need seared along the pathway from the stinging tip to the most sensitive point at the juncture of her thighs.

'And at other times it's like this…'

With his mouth still at the tip of her breast, her let his hand drift downwards. Lingering for a moment at the curve of her waist, he traced a delicate circle around the indenture of her navel, before sliding with practised confidence into the hot, moist cleft hidden among the cluster of dark curling hair.

'Keir!'

His name was a raw, distraught cry of need, a primal sound that she couldn't have held back if she had tried. The wild, burning rush of pleasure that took possession of her pushed her beyond the edges of her control and into a tempestuous, uncivilised territory, where nothing she had ever experienced in the past mattered any more.

'Keir, please!'

Her arms curved around the powerful strength of his back, frantic fingers clenching over his broad shoulders, her nails digging into his skin in mute demand. She wanted him now. Needed to feel him deep inside her, filling her, assuaging the white-hot hunger that burned through every awakened cell in her body.

'Tell me what you want, darling.' Keir's voice was rough with a hunger that matched her own. 'I promised you—anything you want…whatever you want. So tell me…'

'You *know* what I want!'

Restlessly she adjusted her position so that he lay between her thighs. So near and yet so far from giving her what her hungry body craved.

'I want you.'

But still he tormented her by holding off. Still he waited,

watching her face, glittering dark eyes blazing down into hers.

'Say my name, Sienna,' he growled. 'Say it! Say, I want you—Keir.'

She would have said anything he demanded. And why hold back now? After all, it was nothing less than the truth.

'I want you, Keir…'

The words broke on a soaring cry of delight as, with a guttural sound of satisfaction, he moved swiftly, sheathing his strength in her enclosing warmth.

Sienna had barely time to register the glorious sensation of his powerful body filling hers before he began to move. And suddenly she was clinging to him again, beyond thought, beyond knowing even who she was. Every atom of her being was concentrated on the primitive thrusting rhythm that took her out of the known world and lifted her high onto the edge of some undiscovered whirling vortex.

She reached the centre in an explosion of stars, and then suddenly she was crying his name out loud and tumbling, spiralling in a crazy freefall of sensation in which there was no time or space but only herself and Keir and the shattering ecstasy they had created between them.

Above her she felt Keir's powerful body clench, heard his raw cry as he reached his own release before he collapsed on top of her, his broad chest heaving, slowly, slowly coming back down to earth.

It was the start of a very long night. A prolonged, repetitive cycle of awakening desire growing into burning passion, and from there into a frenzied giving and taking of pleasure in all the ways they could think of until at last, satiated and exhausted, the slept in each other's arms, oblivious to the sun coming up, the growing heat of the day.

At that last moment before she finally slid into the depths of sleep, Sienna stirred slightly, managing to lift her head to look into Keir's dark, clouded eyes.

'I'll say one thing for you, husband mine,' she murmured, stretching languorously against him. 'There's no way I could fault you in the performance of those particular conjugal duties.'

She was too tired, too replete, to notice the faint stiffening of the long muscular body beside her. Unaware of the momentary effort he made to bring his thoughts and feelings once more under strict control.

'I aim to please,' he returned, with a carefully casual intonation. 'I promised you a honeymoon to remember. You can believe me when I say that I fully intend to keep that promise.'

CHAPTER SEVEN

'I CAN'T believe I'm really here!' Sienna exclaimed, staring round her in amazement, her mind whirling with the effort of trying to take everything in. 'I can't believe I'm actually in Siena at last.'

Out of the corner of her eye she saw how Keir's mouth twisted slightly, and knew that he was clearly thinking along the same lines as her. There was no way either of them could deny the fact that one of the reasons for the delay between their arrival in Tuscany and the actual visit to Siena itself was the way that they had found it almost impossible to get out of bed.

After that first passion-drenched night, in which they had discovered the mutual delight that their bodies could share, they had indulged again and again in the heady pleasures of the flesh. When they hadn't been making love they had been sleeping off the excesses of the night, just occasionally finding the energy and the inclination to seek the necessary sustenance of food or a cooling, restorative swim in the villa's pool.

But that wasn't all the story. Along with the sensual indulgence of the past ten days had gone Keir's determination that the planned trip to Siena was not to be snatched at too quickly.

'You mustn't gobble the main treat down whole,' he'd reproved gently when, realising that almost half of the allotted days of their honeymoon had passed, Sienna had been desperate to visit the city that had meant so much to her mother. 'You need to take your time, get a feel for the rest of Tuscany too. Believe me, anticipation is a vital part of the enjoyment.' The warm curve to his mouth, the light in his eyes, had told her that he was not just thinking of her expectations of the visit, but other, more intimate pleasures.

And so they had explored other parts of the country together. They had visited such obvious sights as Pisa, with its leaning tower on the green lawns of the Campo dei Miracoli, and Florence, where they had taken in the cathedral, the famous Uffizi gallery and, at the end of a long, steep climb, the beautiful medieval church of San Miniato.

They had crossed the river Arno by the Ponte Vecchio, marvelling at the jewellery in the shops that lined it, and Keir had encouraged Sienna to taste some of the one hundred different variations of ice cream that contributed to Florence's claim to be the ice cream capital of the world. On other occasions they had lingered for hours over coffee or glasses of good red Chianti in some of the many fine restaurants, and Sienna had enjoyed those times as much as any. The slow, desultory conversations they had shared had helped her to relax, to allow herself to believe that perhaps, after all, this fabrication of a marriage might actually work out.

'It all seems so timeless, so unchanging,' she said now. 'It must have looked exactly like this when my mother was here.'

'Well, I don't suppose that twenty-six years or so means very much to a city whose palaces were built according to ideas laid down in the thirteenth century,' Keir returned on a note of amusement. 'With a history like that, the odd quarter of a century must seem like little more than the blink of an eye.'

'Being here now, I can believe that—and yet it's all of my lifetime.'

'Sometimes things change very slowly; sometimes they happen in an instant,' Keir commented cryptically, thinking of the impact she had had on him in the moment they had first met. He had been knocked completely off balance mentally, in the blink of an eyelid, and he had been unable to recover ever since.

Simply to look at her as she was now, tall and slim in a sleeveless turquoise sundress that matched the colour of those amazing eyes, made his body tighten in hungry response. With her dark hair tumbling loose around her shoulders, long, tanned bare legs revealed by her provocatively short skirt, delicate strappy sandals on her feet, she had only to smile in his direction and his temperature shot skywards.

He regretted the revealing comment as Sienna swung round to face him, her eyes bright with frank curiosity.

'That's a very enigmatic comment. Are you thinking of anything in particular?'

Keir's dark eyes wouldn't meet her enquiring turquoise ones as his gesture took in their surroundings in Siena's main square.

'If we'd been here a little earlier in the month, we could have seen the Palio—the horse race held in this square. All the riders and officials dress up in medieval costumes. It's an amazing spectacle.'

It was obvious that she was being distracted from what was actually in his thoughts, but Sienna found that genuine interest got the better of her wanting to pursue that original subject.

'A horse race? *Here?*' Once more she surveyed the uneven shape of the Campo, slightly sloping and irregular, and surrounded on all sides by high buildings of glowing rose-coloured brick. 'It doesn't seem possible—or very wise.'

'The stones are sanded over and the walls are padded. Even so, there are plenty of stories of jockeys—or even horses—flying through the air. But the Sienese say that no one has ever been killed at a Palio. That's because it's supposed to be under the direct protection of the Virgin Mary, but perhaps the fact that the race itself only lasts for a minute and a half has something to do with it.'

'It sounds quite terrifying.' Sienna found it hard to imagine the noise and the excitement of such an event in the sleepy atmosphere of this quiet morning.

'Did your mother never see the Palio? After all, she was

here in June, and the first of the races is run on the second of July.'

'No, she never... How did you know exactly when my mother was here?'

Keir's grin was wide in response to her mystified expression.

'She told me she named you for the place and the month in which you were conceived, and I learned your full name—Sienna June—at the wedding ceremony, of course. We go this way,' he added, catching hold of her hand and leading her down one of the shadowy streets at the west side of the square. 'How did she meet your father?'

Sienna forced herself to ignore the by now so familiar quickening of her pulse that was her automatic response to the touch of his hand on hers. Simply to have his long, hard fingers coiled around her own flooded her body with a glowing warmth that had nothing to do with the heat of the day. Casually dressed, in a white short-sleeved shirt and lightweight black trousers, and with his golden tan enhanced by days in the Italian sun, his tall, lean body had a sensual impact that took her breath away.

'Mum was nanny to a wealthy Sienese family, and my father was here on business—he was a wine importer. They met when he came to dinner with the Lorenzettis. He charmed her, and she fell head over heels in love.'

'He never let on that he was married?'

'Not for a moment.' Sienna shook her dark head in disbelief. 'Mum never suspected a thing until she discovered she was pregnant and he refused to have anything to do with her and the baby—with me.'

Keir's comment on that fact was short, succinct and very rude, making it only too plain how he viewed the selfishness Andrew Nash had displayed.

'He took advantage of her naïveté. She was only—what?—twenty-one?'

'Twenty-two.'

Sienna's response was low-voiced. She was uncomfortably aware of the fact that, although her mother had had the excuse of youth on her side, she herself had been older, infinitely more worldly-wise, when she had met Dean. And yet he had still deceived her just as easily as her father had her mother. More so, in fact. Because not only had he had a wife and a child back home in Brighton, but he had also been seeing someone else, one of Sienna's workmates at the beauty salon.

'Where are we going?'

She forced the question out in order to distract herself from the distress that thinking of Dean caused. She couldn't believe she had let herself be conned in that way. Had always believed that, with her mother's story as a warning always in her mind, she had developed a natural scepticism and instinctive distrust of men who were intent only on trying it on. And yet she had succumbed to Dean's blandishments, his outrageous compliments, his apparent devotion, with the sort of blind foolishness that she now found impossible to believe.

She had swallowed every one of his lies and been enticed into breaking her own careful rules for self-preservation, seduced into his bed with the ease of a practised angler landing a very gullible fish.

'This is Via del Capitano. It leads to the *Duomo*—the cathedral. I warn you, you'll either love it or hate it—there's no in between.'

'You're right!' Sienna could only gasp a short time later as she stared in amazement at the effect of the black and white stripes of marble stretching from floor to ceiling in the nave and the aisles of the huge Gothic cathedral. 'It's amazing! It looks like nothing so much as a huge mint humbug!'

She was thankful to find the cathedral so fascinating, grateful for the opportunity it gave her to be distracted from the pain of her memories. She was able to push all thoughts of Dean from her mind until at last they wandered back down into the centre of Siena, to lunch on bread and cheese and black olives, sitting in the sun on the pavement outside a small *trattoria*.

'I'm surprised your mother didn't name you Catherine, after Siena's very own saint,' Keir commented, breaking off a crust of bread and spreading it liberally with butter. 'After all, she was born not so very far from here—on Vicolo del Tiratoio.'

'She said she thought about it, but as a name it didn't have the special significance that Siena had for her, though in the end she decided she preferred a slightly different spelling. You know, this is totally crazy!'

Intrigued by her tone, Keir looked up, brown eyes frowning into the sun.

'What is?' he enquired mildly.

'All this talk of my mother and her past, when I know nothing about yours—and I'm married to you!'

Broad shoulders under the immaculate white shirt lifted in a dismissive shrug.

'There's nothing much to tell,' Keir stated off-handedly.

'I don't believe that. A man with your looks—your money—there must have been women...'

'There have—plenty of them.' It was an emotionless statement offered in a flat tone that erased any suspicion of boasting. 'But no one who really mattered.'

'You never fell in love?'

'Love?' He seemed to be considering the word, his expression thoughtful as he sipped at his wine. 'Rick Parry always says that my one true love is my work. And I suppose in a way it was true. Certainly from the time that I came back from university to discover that Dad had almost reduced Alexander's to the state where the next step would have been to call in the receivers, getting the firm back on its feet again was something of an obsession. Any women in my life took strictly second place.'

He didn't sound in the least bit penitent about it, Sienna reflected. Instead, his almost casual delivery spoke of indifference to the effect his actions might have had.

'So there was no one special?'

'There was one girl I thought I cared for more than all the rest.' Keir swirled the wine round in his glass, staring down into its ruby depths. 'But when it came down to it, I cared about my work more.'

'It strikes me she had a lucky escape!'

Those dark-chocolate eyes lifted to meet Sienna's blue-green gaze, and Keir's sensual mouth twisted at the indignation in her tone.

'What I felt for her wasn't the real thing.'

'And would you know the *real thing* if it bit you on the nose?'

'If I'd truly loved her, then nothing else would have mattered. I would have given her all the time she needed, given up work—even the company—to be with her.'

Which put her right in her place, Sienna told herself bitterly. He hadn't been prepared to give anything up for her. On the contrary, the only reason he had married her was in order to obtain the money he needed to save that precious company of his. She didn't even rank as highly as the girl he'd thought he'd cared for.

'So what about you?'

'What about me?' Still struggling at the smart of facing up to just how little she truly meant to Keir, Sienna didn't trouble to adjust her tone, earning herself a quick, dark frown of reproof.

'Are you going to tell me the gory details of your love-life?'

'Nothing to tell.' She aimed for airy insouciance and missed it by a mile, fingers clenching tight over her knife until her knuckles showed white.

'Not even about your precious Dean?'

The sarcasm of the question caught Sienna on the raw. Turquoise eyes flashing angrily, she lifted her head and glared defiance straight into his still, watchful face.

'Dean is none of your business!'

'I'm making it my business,' Keir shot back. 'Dean hurt you and humiliated you...'

She didn't need reminding of that! But what shocked and stunned her into blank confusion was a new realisation, that came with a rush that made her head spin dizzily.

Dean had beguiled and seduced her. He had enticed her into his bed with soft words and softer lies, and, foolishly, crazily in love with him, she had offered no resistance. But never once in all that time that she and Dean had been lovers had she ever experienced the sheer mind-blowing, soul-shattering physical ecstasy that she had known with Keir since their wedding day.

She had never been able to respond to Dean as she did to Keir, never wanted him as she wanted this man who was now her husband. And Dean's lovemaking had never left her exhausted and satiated, yet knowing that he had only to touch her and her whole body would come alive once again, desperately yearning, needing more.

'It's nothing to do with you!'

'You're my wife.'

'Your *wife*!' Sienna echoed, pain shading her words with black cynicism. 'And we both know just how much—or rather how little—that means, husband dear.'

'I'm a better damn husband than your precious Dean would ever have been, sweetheart! Would he have brought you here, to Siena? Would he have provided this honey-moon?'

'You didn't have to lay on a honeymoon! No one asked you to!'

She regretted the impetuous words as soon as they had left her lips, urgently wishing them back as she saw the black scowl that darkened his handsome features.

'You're wrong there, my lovely Sienna,' Keir put in, his coldly clipped enunciation freezing the impulse to apologise before it had time to fully form. 'I may only be the husband you hired on a temporary basis, but, believe me, I know what's expected of me. And I have every intention of fulfilling my contract to the letter.'

'Keir, please. You know you're—'

'Know I'm what? More than that? Don't kid yourself, darling—and don't try to pretend to me because it won't work. But one thing I do know…'

Pushing back his chair so violently that it scraped over the pavement with an ugly grating sound, Keir got to his feet in a swift, angry movement.

'One thing I'll never be is second best—not to your precious Dean, or anyone else. And if you want proof…'

'Keir…' Sienna, tried but her voice failed her as he moved to her side, towering over her threateningly, a wild, dangerous look in his coffee-coloured eyes. 'I…'

Her second feeble attempt at remonstration went unheeded as Keir reached down and clamped powerful fingers on her arms, pulling her out of her seat and yanking her close up against the hard strength of his body. She was lifted half off her feet, only the very tips of her toes still retaining contact with the ground as she swayed against him. With one arm holding her tight, his other hand came under her chin, forcing her face up to meet his as his mouth swooped downwards.

In such a public place, his kiss was almost shocking in its fierce sensuality. Instantly a river of golden heat raged through every nerve and cell in Sienna's body, sending her thoughts spinning off into a wild fever over which she had no control at all, her mind hazing as if she was in the grip of some delirium. Her soul seemed to be drawn out of her body, the electrical current of need that pulsed at the centre of her being making her whimper with a hunger that was dangerously close to pain.

It was several moments before she became aware of anything other that Keir. And it was only when she was released and set down, blinking hard in the sudden brightness of the sunlight, that she became aware of the interested and very approving audience his actions had earned for them.

'Now tell me I'm second best,' Keir challenged menacingly. 'Tell me your Dean can match that.'

And when she could only shake her head, her eyes glazed with desire, unable to speak, his smile was positively fiendish in its dark triumph.

'I thought not. Forget Dean, Sienna. He's the past—gone. I am your present, and you are mine—for this year at least. And I'll have no third party intruding into this marriage. Is that understood?'

'Understood,' was all that Sienna managed to croak in reply.

'Good.'

With a gesture of supreme arrogance, Keir tossed down a handful of notes in payment of their bill before linking his hand with hers so firmly that, even if she had thought of resistance, she would have had no chance of getting away.

'And now, my lovely wife, we're going home. Back to the villa and to our bedroom, where I will prove to you once more that I am all the husband you need.'

He didn't give her a chance to argue, obviously not expecting any hint of objection from her. And the problem was, Sienna reflected, she was incapable of making any. The excitement his kiss had aroused still spiralled deep inside her, fed by the anticipation of just what awaited her when they reached the villa.

Feeling like this, she admitted to herself, she would go anywhere Keir asked her to, do anything he commanded. Somehow over the past ten days he had enslaved her sexually, and right now she doubted if she could possibly break free of his sensual mastery ever again.

CHAPTER EIGHT

'SIENNA, darling, do you know that there's still a film in here?'

'Hmm?' Frowning distractedly, Sienna dragged her attention away from the list she had been studying. 'I'm sorry, Mum, what did you say?'

'I wanted to know if you'd realised that there's a film in this camera.'

Caroline Rushford waved the article in question under her daughter's nose.

'Do you know when it was last used?'

'Oh. . .'

Sienna chewed the end of her pen as she thought about answering. Not because she needed time to think, but for exactly the opposite reason. She was only too well aware of when anyone had last taken a photograph with that particular camera, just as she knew precisely why it had been put away with the film unfinished rather than taken to be developed.

'That'll be the camera I took on honeymoon,' she said carefully.

'But that's over three months ago! I would have thought you'd have wanted to see the pictures you'd taken before now.'

'I—forgot about it. There's been a lot going on.'

'But your *honeymoon*, darling! Surely you and Keir would want to look back at the pictures and remember?'

That was precisely what she *didn't* want to do, Sienna reflected privately. She still couldn't look back at the days she had spent in Italy with Keir without feeling distinctly uncomfortable. And, even after three months, she still wasn't prepared to contemplate any evidence of that time, even if only in a photograph.

She felt that she had lost something of herself while she had been away. Or did she mean she'd found a side of herself she hadn't known existed? She didn't know and couldn't begin to work it out. All she did know was that she had gone to Italy as one woman and come home another.

And that woman was addicted to Keir Alexander.

There was no other way to describe how Keir made her feel. He was in her blood, in her mind, in her *soul*. When he was with her, she couldn't keep away from him, but was constantly drawn to his side as a needle to the most powerful magnet. She had to watch every expression that crossed his stunning face, every movement of his sexy body. Her hands, too, wouldn't stay by her side but had to keep reaching out, touching his shoulder or his arm, her fingers tangling with his.

And when he wasn't there—which, she had to admit, was more likely the case these days—she missed him unbearably. The emptiness of the space where he should have been was like a reproach to her, the feeling of incompleteness she felt like an ache in the very core of her being. It was as if some part of her, an arm or a leg, had been amputated and she hadn't yet learned how to function without it.

The only time she felt fully whole was when she was in bed with him. When his arms were round her, his mouth on her skin, his powerful body linked possessively with hers…

'Smile!'

Sienna started nervously, her head coming up, eyes blinking frantically as she reacted to a sudden, unexpected flash of light.

Her consternation grew as a whirring sound from the camera revealed that the film was now used up, and the rewind mechanism had come into operation.

'Mum, what—?'

'There was only one frame left, so I took your picture to finish it. You looked like a startled rabbit, but who cares! Now you can take the film to be developed and we can all have a look at the honeymoon photos.'

'There won't be time,' Sienna objected. 'We have too much packing to do.'

The alterations to her father's house had been completed, and they were due to move out of Keir's apartment and into their new home by the end of the following week.

'And just how long does it take to drop a film in at the shop? We're only moving house, Sienna, not leaving the country! And if you won't have time, then I'll get Keir to do it.'

'If you can catch him.' Sienna's tone was dry, blending into cynical. 'I don't think he's been home before ten once this month.'

And on several nights it had been well past midnight before she had heard the sound of his car drawing up outside, his key being inserted in the lock. On those late nights she had made herself go to bed, hating the thought of Keir finding her still up and waiting for him. She had even tried to force herself to sleep, but had been unable to do so.

On the one rare occasion when, exhausted by a very long day of organising and packing, she had actually drifted into a light doze she had woken instantly at the feel of him sliding in beside her. He hadn't even needed to touch her. Just the faint sound he'd made, the scent of his skin reaching her, had had her turning to him, her body raging with a hunger that would have been far more appropriate if they had been apart for fourteen days instead of as many hours.

'Yes, he does seem to be working very hard.' Caroline frowned her concern. 'There isn't any problem, is there?'

'What sort of problem?'

It was impossible to erase the uneasy edge from her voice. Had she put a foot wrong somewhere, so that her mother had begun to suspect the truth about her marriage? Had Caroline, after three months of seeing her daughter and son-in-law together at the close quarters necessitated by their sharing the same house, come to realise that it was not, after all, the love match she believed?

'Oh, not between you two—that's obvious! Anyone who's not completely blind can see that you're absolutely besotted and that you can't keep your hands off each other.'

'Mum!'

'Now don't go coy on me!' Caroline laughed, regarding her daughter's flaming cheeks with an indulgent smile. 'I may be middle-aged, and a bit wobbly on my pins, but I hope my mind is still as broad as it ever was. I would have more to worry about if you and Keir *didn't* fancy the pants off each other, seeing as you're still such newly-weds. No, it was Keir's job I was thinking of. There isn't anything wrong at Alexander's, is there?'

'Nothing I know of,' Sienna hastened to assure her.

Not that she knew much more than her mother. The only time Keir had ever really talked to her about his company had been in the days before their marriage, when his account of Lucille's hostile negotiations had first put the idea of proposing into her head.

But once the wedding ceremony had been performed, and she had signed the documents he had produced so precipitately at the reception, he had never said another word on the subject. Alexander's success or failure was a closed book as far as she was concerned.

'You know Keir. The original workaholic, that's my husband.'

'Well, see if you can't get him to ease up a bit. I'm surprised you haven't made some sort of protest at the way he's neglecting you. It's not good for a husband to work so hard in the first months of marriage.'

Caroline shot her daughter an arch glance.

'After all, you don't want him too tired when he gets home, do you?'

'Mum, really!'

'Oh, don't give me that look, Sienna! I can still remember

how it felt to be head over heels in love, even if for me it didn't work out as well as it has for you and Keir. Which reminds me...'

Reaching for the camera again, she opened the back and took out the finished roll of film.

'I can't wait to see your pictures of Siena.' The faint shimmer of tears in her blue eyes betrayed just how much it meant to her. 'So promise me you'll get this developed as soon as possible.'

Did she have any alternative? Sienna asked herself. How could she possibly turn her mother down?

'Of course I will,' she sighed. 'I'll take care of it first thing tomorrow.'

'And tell that husband of yours to ease up. I'm sure he doesn't have to spend quite so much time at the office.'

'My mother's worried about you,' Sienna flung the words at Keir as soon as he came into their bedroom later that night.

Much later, she registered with a strange sense of unease. In a series of late nights, this was one of the latest. Just what did Keir find to do until almost midnight almost every night?

'She thinks you're working too hard.'

'And good evening to you, too,' Keir returned satirically, slumping down onto the end of the bed and tugging his tie free at his throat.

My mother's worried about you! This wife of his really knew how to stick a knife in without appearing to do so. Her mother! Did she know what it did to him to come home and find his wife in his bed, wearing only the sexiest slip of a nightgown he had ever seen, and be told that *her mother* worried about him? Which begged the implication that Sienna herself didn't give a damn.

'So do you agree with her?'

The narrow-eyed look he turned on her had a disturbingly

appraising quality about it, one that made Sienna shift uneasily under the soft, downy duvet.

She was painfully aware of the fact that she was wearing only an oyster-coloured silk nightdress, its deep vee neckline exposing more of the creamy curves of her breasts than she was comfortable with in the present situation. Keir on the other hand was still fully dressed in an exquisitely cut dark grey suit, white shirt and what had once been an elegant burgundy silk tie but which was now hopelessly mangled by the careless way he was pulling at it.

'You have been staying out late a lot.'

'I'm a grown man, Sienna. I stopped obeying a night-time curfew on my eighteenth birthday.'

'I realise that. But would it be asking too much for you to let me know when you're going to be really late?'

'Why, sweetheart?' It was a soft, silky hiss. The sort of voice that the serpent must have used in the Garden of Eden. 'Missed me have you?'

'Of course not!'

The retort had come too swiftly, Sienna reproached herself. It had been far too vehement as well.

'I know you can look after yourself,' she amended hastily. Understatement of the year. He could more than look after himself. She couldn't imagine anyone who, coming under the influence of that charisma, the aura of authority and total self-assurance that he wore with the ease of a natural right, would even dare to *think* of trying it on.

'Then what's the problem?'

He was tugging at his tie again, his movements rough and impatient. When it finally came loose in his hand he tossed it in the vague direction of a chair, totally ignoring the way it fell short, slithering onto the thick bronze carpet instead.

'I—she—we were afraid you'd wear yourself out.'

Even as she spoke the words she saw how ridiculous they were. She'd rarely, if ever, seen Keir even slightly tired, never mind worn out. He was one of those men who seemed to have endless reserves of stamina and was able to pace himself perfectly. When other, weaker people were falling by the wayside he just kept on going, never looking hurried or flustered, always in control.

'How very thoughtful of you.' Keir's tone said exactly the opposite.

He was shrugging himself out of his jacket now, the elegant garment following the tie in the direction of the chair, with rather more success this time. No sooner had it landed than Keir pushed off his shoes, not even bothering to unfasten the laces first, then moved to lounge against the pillows on his side of the bed, legs stretched out before him, crossed at the ankles.

'So what's the problem, darling? Are you not getting enough?'

'No!' It was an indignant squawk. 'I mean… I…'

Sienna struggled to collect her whirling thoughts. But it was hard—almost impossible—to concentrate on what she was trying to say. Sprawled beside her, his long body indolently at ease, Keir had now begun to unbutton his shirt, displaying a tantalising amount of smoothly muscled chest, the tanned skin hazed with fine dark hair. Just the sight of it dried Sienna's mouth painfully, so that she had to swallow convulsively to ease the tightness in her throat.

Dear God, was he planning on doing a complete striptease? He was so close to her that the warm scent of his body, subtly mixed with the clean, crisp tang of the cologne he wore, tantalised her nostrils. Did he have any awareness of the effect he was having on her? The way that her heart now beat in double-quick time, her blood singing a restless incantation of delight in her veins?

But then Keir slanted a lazy, heavy-lidded glance in her direction, and, seeing the provocative gleam in the dark-chocolate colour of his eyes, she recognised that of course he knew what he was doing. Knew it and was playing on it quite deliberately, aiming for just the effect he had created.

'Are you sure?' he teased now, his voice low and rich so

that it made her think of dark honey running smoothly over gravel. 'Because I wouldn't want my precious bride to feel that she was being short-changed. If I'm skimping on my husbandly duties...'

'Oh, to hell with your husbandly duties!' Sienna exploded in exasperation. 'Why do you have to bring everything down to sex?'

Keir's dark eyes rounded in a display of hurt innocence that was so obviously make-believe Sienna had to grit her teeth against the impulse to lash out and wipe it from his handsome face.

'Did I mention sex, darling?' he asked, his tone as wounded as his expression. 'I don't believe the word ever crossed my lips. But if that's what this is all about...'

'You know very well that it's nothing of the sort!' Sienna flashed, moving swiftly to one side to dodge the kiss he was clearly planning on planting on her mouth.

She knew only too well what would happen if she let him touch her. One kiss and she would go up in flames. The potent sensuality that he could trigger with just one caress would swamp her mind, leaving her incapable of thought. And then tonight would follow the same voluptuous pattern as every other night of their marriage. He would take her down the entrancing paths she had come to know so well, give her the physical delights that she craved so greedily, reduce her to an exhausted, satiated wreck, and any opportunity to talk would be lost.

'I'm not the one with a cesspit for a mind.'

The mocking angle of one straight black brow clearly questioned the truth of that unwise declaration, a wicked, derisive smile curving the corners of Keir's mouth.

'What I meant was...'

She couldn't complete the sentence; her mind totally distracted by the sight of Keir pulling open the narrow leather belt at the waistband of his trousers in order to free his shirt completely.

Under cover of the bedclothes, she clenched her hands

into such tight, rigid fists that her nails dug painfully into her palms. It was either that or give in to the appalling temptation to touch. To push aside the soft white material and let her wanton fingers explore the warm, tight contours of his muscles, the hard frame of his chest.

'What you meant was…?' Keir prompted softly as she swallowed hard.

'What I meant was…' Sienna struggled to ignore his wicked, sexy grin. 'Is everything all right—at work. Is there some problem with Alexander's?'

If she had thrown a bucket of icy water right in his face she couldn't have destroyed the seductive mood any more completely. Keir's face froze, carved features hardening into rigid rejection, his eyes taking on an obsidian glitter that made them look like dark shards of ice.

'That's my business!' he snapped coldly, jack-knifing out of his relaxed pose and into a stiffly upright position, every tight muscle in his long frame speaking with dangerous eloquence of the strength of his rejection of her. 'My business and mine alone.'

The force of his reaction startled and worried Sienna. Was her mother right after all? Did the long hours that Keir had been working mean that, in spite of the injection of cash she had made into Alexander's, the company was still in difficulties? She knew how much that company meant to Keir. It was his only link with his late father, and she couldn't bear to contemplate the effect losing it would have on him.

'But it isn't just your business,' she protested, flinging back the bedclothes and reaching for the silk robe, an exact match for her nightdress, which lay across the foot of the bed.

She would feel much more in control if she covered up, she told herself as she belted it tightly around her slim waist. A seductive sliver of silk and lace might be suitable for a passionate night; it was totally inappropriate for a serious business meeting.

'I'm involved in Alexander's too.'

Could he ever forget it? Keir asked himself. All these months ago, on a mad, foolish impulse, he had snatched at the offer she'd made him, seeing it as his only way out of a tricky situation. Alexander's or Sienna. The woman or the company. That had seemed to be the choice he'd been faced with then.

If he put in the concentrated effort his company needed, then he would have to neglect his relationship with the woman who had knocked him for six in the moment he'd first seen her. And everything about her attitude had said that if he did just that then she wasn't likely to stay around for long. But if he went with his emotional instincts, and focused solely on his developing feelings for Sienna, then Lucille would make her move and he could lose everything.

And then Sienna had come up with the astonishing proposal that had seemed to be the answer to all his problems. He could rescue Alexander's and at the same time win himself a breathing space with Sienna. At the time, the year she had declared their marriage should last had seemed like an eternity—more than enough time to win her round, seduce her into wanting him, needing him, and, hopefully, falling in love with him so that they could turn their temporary marriage into a permanent relationship.

Well, he'd sorted the work problems. More than sorted them. After three months' concentrated effort, Alexander's was well and truly back on track, with the potential to be even more successful than ever.

But three months with Sienna seemed to have had no effect at all. If anything, it seemed he was further from winning her heart than when he'd first started. Oh, she *wanted* him; there was no doubt about that. The physical side of their relationship was everything he'd ever dreamed it would be, and then some! But sex was all it was. There was no trace of a possibility that she had come to care for him at all.

And if he'd needed any further proof of that, then she'd

just thrown it right into his face. Just the suspicion of any problem on the financial front and she'd switched immediately from bedroom to boardroom mode. Though he supposed he ought to be grateful for the fact that she'd put on her robe. At least now he'd be able to think straight, without being constantly distracted by the sight of her creamy skin, the rich curves of her breasts.

'What's wrong, Sienna?' Disappointment put a caustic bite into his voice. 'Are you worried about the return on your investment? Afraid that I might actually go under—that you could end up married to a man who isn't as wealthy as you thought? One who may even be *poor*?'

'Is that possible?'

Shock and consternation showed in her face. How could this have happened? Could she really have been so blind that she hadn't noticed the difficulties Keir was facing?

But of course she had. She'd been only too aware of the long hours he was working, the length of his absences from the house. She just hadn't realised the reasons for them. Instead she had attributed his preoccupation to a need to be away from her, to put a distance between them. How could she have been so stupid—so selfish!

'Keir, are things really so bad?'

'Depends on what you're looking for,' Keir returned laconically.

Stretching lazily, he linked his hands behind his head, leaning back against them and half closing his eyes. The movement pulled his shirt open wider over his chest and the way his heavy eyelids drooped at the outer corners gave him a sleepily sensual look that tugged at her heart with disturbing appeal.

'If you want to be married to a man who can match your father's money pound for pound, then stick around, you might strike lucky. But if you're looking for a way out of our agreement, then tough—no deal, lady.'

'Keir, don't be silly!'

Confusion mixed with a half-formed sense of relief to

create an exasperation she couldn't explain. Did he mean that things were okay with Alexander's, or just the opposite? She had no way of knowing, and Keir's body language gave her no help at all.

That apparently indolently relaxed position could be just what it seemed, or it could be a deliberate front, nicely calculated to hide a very different set of feelings, ones he was determined not to let her see.

'Why on earth should I want out of our arrangement? I still need your co-operation, remember! My uncle Francis has only handed over part of my inheritance—the rest of it is dependent on our staying together for the year we agreed on. I have to keep you as my husband until then.'

Well, that's told you, Alexander, you fool! Keir mocked himself. She couldn't have spelled it out any more clearly if she'd tried. And the irony was that just for a moment, a weak, crazy moment, he had actually let the idea of telling her the truth slide into his mind.

What the hell could he have been thinking of? Admitting that he cared for—that he loved—there, now he'd admitted it to himself—a woman who saw him only as the key to her father's fortune? He needed to have his brain examined. Keir could only shake his head in disbelief at his own foolishness. Did he plan to lie down on the floor in front of her and let her walk all over him with those dainty, narrow feet?

'No?'

To his consternation he realised that Sienna had caught his unthinking shake of the head and had interpreted it in a very different way.

'What do you mean, no, Keir?'

Sienna wished she could bring her voice down an octave or two. It sounded far too shrill and accusatory at this pitch. And if she wasn't careful then the high, tight sound might even reach to where her mother lay sleeping at the far end of the corridor.

'Are you trying to say you don't intend sticking by our contract?'

Sienna felt as if her stomach was turning summersaults inside her. What would she do without him? The future suddenly seemed unbearably bleak when viewed from the perspective of having to face it alone.

'Do you want out? Is that it, Keir? Have you…?'

The truth was suddenly unnervingly bright, like a brilliant spotlight concentrated onto previously concealed corners of her mind, illuminating things she would prefer to have kept hidden away.

'Have you found someone? Is that it?'

Just for a moment Keir's gaze slid away from hers, intensifying her unease one thousandfold. He looked decidedly shifty, as if he very definitely had something to hide.

'Have you—have you fallen in love with someone else?'

'Don't be so stupid!' Keir exploded, all traces of the lazy mood burning away in the heat of the dark fury that blazed in his eyes. 'I gave you my word and I intend to stick by that, no matter what!'

'Oh, thank God!'

The rush of relief was so intense that she almost sagged against the side of the bed, and only just disguised the moment of weakness by transforming it into a none too elegant drop onto the padded stool in front of her dressing table.

'Yeah, thank God!' Keir echoed with black cynicism. 'Oh, don't worry, my lovely, your inheritance is quite safe with me! You paid for a year of my life, and that's what you'll get, right down to the very last second.'

Suddenly too restless to stay still any longer, he flung himself to his feet and strode round to where she perched on the stool, her slender arms folded tightly around herself. The wary look in her brilliant eyes as she watched him approach only inflamed further the volatile mixture of emotions he was already prey to.

She didn't trust him; that was the real problem. Didn't trust him not to take the money and run, leaving her in the lurch once again, all alone and with a sick mother to care for. That rat Dean Hanson really had done a number on her!

It was just as well he couldn't get his hands on him right at this moment, because he would be strongly tempted to do something very foolish indeed. And it would be nothing less than the repellent louse deserved!

'That's all I want.'

Sienna's voice was as coolly distant as her expression, but he would never know the effort it had cost her to keep it that way. Keir had looked positively murderous marching towards her just now, and it had been all she could do to keep her composure when every nerve in her body was screaming at her to get off the stool and run. Put as great a distance as possible between the two of them as quickly as possible.

'At least we both know where we stand.'

'So we do.'

His expressive mouth curved into a bleak travesty of a smile, one that had no trace of humour in it and which did nothing at all to warm the arctic bleakness of his eyes.

'But let me just clear up a couple of final points—or rather, correct some misconceptions you seem to hold about just what our original agreement entailed.'

One strong hand was held up between them, only inches away from her face, and Keir's voice was coldly emphatic as he marked off each point on a finger as he made it.

'One—you paid me to marry you; what I do with the money is none of your business. Your investment was in *me*, not Alexander's. Two—the state of my company is no concern of yours, nor will it ever be. I handle my own affairs as I see fit, and I won't answer to you about any of them. And three—I agreed to be a husband, not a lapdog. I'll act like your husband in public, be at your side when you need me, but that's all. I'm not at your beck and call. I come and go as I please, do what I want when I want. Is that understood?'

'Perfectly.' Sienna was proud of her control over her voice as she answered him. It matched his cold enunciation perfectly. So much so that she almost expected to see the letters form in shapes of ice on the carpet between them.

'Because if there's anything there you can't live with, then I suggest we dissolve our partnership right here and now.'

'There's no need for that! What you're offering is precisely what I want from you. Nothing more; nothing less.'

'Then at least we understand each other.'

Keir flexed his broad shoulders, pushing both hands through the dark silk of his hair. The movement ruffled its usual sleek smoothness, causing one wayward lock to fall forward onto his forehead in a way that Sienna found dangerously appealing. Before she had time to think of the possible consequences of her action, she had reached out and brushed it gently back into place.

'Sienna…'

The sound of Keir's voice told her immediately how his mood had changed in an instant. Dropping an octave or more, it had become a huskily sensual whisper, one that curled like smoke around every nerve, making her toes curl in instant response on the soft, thick pile of the carpet. Chocolate-brown eyes locked with aquamarine, and Keir's intent gaze held her mesmerised, unable to look away, incapable even of breathing as she froze into immobility.

'When I came into this room you were decidedly peeved. I have to wonder why you were in such a bad mood?'

'I—I told you why,' Sienna managed with difficulty. 'My mother…'

Keir's arrogant flick of a hand dismissed the mention of Caroline as the irrelevance it was.

'Correct me if I'm wrong, but I suspect you were feeling neglected. "You have been staying out late a lot…"'

Sienna blinked in shock as he mimicked her own petulant tone with distinctly unnerving accuracy. Her sense of disbelief deepened as she saw Keir's smile, the way the pupils of his eyes had enlarged until there was only the tiniest rim of brown at their edges.

'If that's the case, darling, you only have to say. Because if you're not getting what you want...'

One long-fingered hand slid under her chin, lifting her face up towards his, his hard palm warm against her cheek. The temptation to turn her mouth into that palm, press a lingering kiss against it, was almost overwhelming. But then, just as she was about to succumb, a very different thought struck her, changing her mood abruptly.

'I'd be only too happy to put things right. After all, I am your husband...'

'My husband as defined by the strictly narrow business terms you detailed only moments ago!' Sienna flared, wrenching her head away from his beguiling caress.

She refused to allow herself even to register the screaming protest from every awakened nerve in her body as she sprang to her feet, facing him defiantly from a safe distance of several metres.

'This isn't a real marriage, and we both know it!'

'We have a certificate that says otherwise,' Keir pointed out imperturbably.

'But there's a whole lot more to a marriage than just a piece of paper! Important things. Things that make the difference between a union that will last and one that's already past its sell-by date!'

Tell me about it, Keir reflected broodingly. It was the lack of those important things that chafed at him day and night, eating into his heart like acid. His only antidote was work, the long, wearing hours that he spent in the office every day.

Or sex. Only in bed could he express anything of the way he felt for Sienna. And only in bed would she respond in kind.

'Come to bed, Sienna.' He spoke without thinking, cursing his foolish tongue when he saw the stormy rejection in her sea-coloured eyes.

Come to bed! She couldn't believe the arrogance of the man. He had just spelled out to her in no uncertain terms the fact that she meant nothing to him except as part of a purely mercenary deal, and now he thought he could click his fingers and she would jump into bed with him without a second's thought. She had far more respect for herself than that, and even though her wanton body hungered for the feel of his against it she was determined to defy it.

'Sex won't change anything!' she tossed at him, magnificent in her disdain. 'And even a *proper* wife can say no.'

A faint smile touched her lips as she saw his proud head go back in surprise.

'Yes, Keir, I'm saying no to you. Is that a first? Am I the only woman ever to have resisted your all-conquering charms?'

The only one who'd ever mattered. But he'd be damned if he let her see it.

'That's your prerogative, sweetheart.' He smiled, his smile a masterpiece of indifference. 'But if you change your mind, just come and find me.'

'Come and…' He was already halfway towards the door by the time her mind had cleared enough to let her speak. 'But where are you going?'

Keir spared her only the briefest of glances, not even slowing his long, smooth strides.

'I'll sleep in the spare room tonight, darling,' he threw over his shoulder at her. 'I think we'll both find it more comfortable that way.'

Beyond speaking, beyond thought, Sienna could only stand and stare as she watched the door swing to behind him. She was totally unprepared for the rush of distress that assailed her as she heard Keir's angry footsteps moving swiftly down the corridor.

She had meant every word she'd said, so why should she feel so lost, so bereft, so desolated by the way he had left her? Somewhere during the course of tonight the balance of their relationship had shifted disturbingly, leaving her shocked and bewildered by her own response.

She had always known that Keir had only married her for

the money she had offered him. Known that there was no emotion in the role he played, that he was a husband in name only and would never be anything more. It was what she had wanted from him after all. So why should that suddenly prove to be so out of synch with her feelings? Why did his indifference now have the power to hurt her so terribly?

CHAPTER NINE

SHE got her answer just thirty-six hours later.

If she was honest with herself, Sienna had to admit that she'd known all along. But she couldn't bring herself to acknowledge the truth, even to herself. It created too many problems, complicated things impossibly. And the consequences for her own future were more than she dared to contemplate.

But when she saw the photograph she knew, absolutely and finally, without any hope of redemption. There was no denying anything any more. No way of dodging round the truth. It was there, right in front of her, as clear as day.

'Oh, no!' she whispered weakly, fighting against the tears that burned in her eyes. 'How could this have happened? And what on earth do I do now?'

She hadn't been able to get out of taking the photographs to be developed. Her mother had insisted on it.

'And make sure you ask for the twenty-four hour service!' she'd added as Sienna had reluctantly left the house to carry out the errand. 'I've waited over three months to see those pictures. I don't intend to delay any longer!'

And of course the first thing she'd done this morning was to remind her daughter to collect the prints just as soon as she could.

She didn't really understand what instinct had driven her to open the package of photographs as soon as she'd got back to her car. If pressed, she would have said that seeing them was the last thing she wanted right then. After the argument she had had with Keir, her thoughts had been so unsettled, her mood swinging violently from one extreme to another, that the last thing she needed was any more to worry about.

Keir had come home later than ever last night. So late that she had no idea of what time he had actually arrived home. She had waited and waited for him, but in the end exhaustion had got the better of her and she had fallen fast asleep. In fact, the only indication she'd had that he'd been in the house at all had been the indentation left by his head in the pillow beside her when she'd woken, and the discovery of the clothes he had worn that day lying discarded in the washing basket.

By the time she'd surfaced from a restless and unsatisfying sleep he'd already gone. She had had no chance to see him, hadn't spoken to him since he had walked out on her the night before last.

So it had been the foolish thought that she desperately needed to see his face, even if only in the flat, one-dimensional form of a photograph, that had driven her to wrench open the envelope and pull out its contents.

It was the first one she saw. Lying on top of the pile, clear and crisply defined, undeniable in its impact, the picture had a shock value that winged straight into her heart, like an arrow thudding into the gold at the centre of a target.

She remembered the scene only too well. It had been on the afternoon of their visit to Florence, when she and Keir had made their way through the narrow, straight streets around the Piazza della Repubblica to the Mercato Nuovo.

'You can't leave Florence without seeing Il Porcellino,' Keir had announced.

'Il Porcellino? The piglet?' Sienna was proud of her growing knowledge of the Italian language. 'What on earth is that?'

And when she was confronted by the large bronze statue she exclaimed in amused surprise.

'That's no *piglet*! It's a fully-grown boar!' she said, eyeing the strong body, the dangerous looking tusks at either side of the snout. The end of the creature's nose looked more polished than the rest of him, rubbed smooth and shiny, obviously by much handling.

'You have to rub his snout,' Keir told her, a grin surfacing in response to her bemused expression. 'Go on,' he urged, when she hesitated.

Unable to resist that smile, Sienna had done as he asked, looking up at Keir for an answer as she did so.

'Can you tell me exactly *why* I'm doing this? I presume it has some special significance?'

Keir nodded his dark head in response. 'It's supposed to bring good luck, but more especially make sure that one day destiny will bring you back to Florence again in the future.'

'Oh, well, in that case…'

Sienna rubbed the bronze muzzle once again, with renewed enthusiasm.

'I've fallen in love with Italy, with Tuscany in particular, and I'd love to come back to this beautiful city any time fate wants to bring me here.'

It was the uncomfortable little skip of her heart, making her breath catch unexpectedly in the middle of the sentence, that warned her. Suddenly she couldn't take her eyes from Keir, standing so tall and strong just to one side. His casual elegance, in a black polo shirt and smart chinos, had a heart-stopping impact, but what suddenly made her shiver, in spite of the heat, was what she saw in his eyes.

The smile on that handsome face seemed strangely forced and unnatural, and the dark pools of his eyes remained bleak and shadowed, no warmth lighting them at all.

One day destiny will bring you back to Florence again in the future. Yes, but *when* in the future, and with whom? In twelve month's time she and Keir would be divorced, and would probably never see each other again.

Sienna shivered again, a cold, creeping sensation slithering down her spine. She couldn't imagine ever coming here without Keir. His presence was so much a part of her enjoyment of the place, her delight in Tuscany, that she couldn't think of it without him.

'Keir!'

Impulsively she reached out and caught hold of his hand, pulling him forward.

'You must do it too! You must stroke Porcellino's snout!'

When for a moment it seemed that he would resist, that he would refuse to move, she felt the faint feeling of unease grow worse, developing into a disturbing near-panic that made her heart race.

'Keir!' she tried again, disconcerted to find her voice quavering on his name. 'Don't you want to come back to Florence? I can't believe that!'

At last he moved, stepping forward and giving the bronze boar a desultory pat on the muzzle.

'*Ciao*, Porcellino,' he said, and it was the cool flippancy of the response that told Sienna just what had been going through his mind.

He didn't care whether he came back to Florence or not. He was totally indifferent to the fact. Or rather, he didn't care if he never came back *with her*.

And now, all these months later, Sienna was confronted by the evidence of just what that had meant to her. Lying in her lap, where her nerveless fingers had dropped it, was a photograph of herself in the Mercato Nuovo, her hand still resting lightly on the bronze statue of the boar.

She remembered exactly when it had been taken. While she had struggled with the unsettled thoughts Keir's response had brought to her mind, he had stepped back quite coolly, and, with a casual command of 'Smile!', had captured her image before she'd had time to protest.

He had captured much more than that too. Sienna sighed, looking into the image of her own face. He had caught her look of uncertainty, the confusion as she'd struggled with her thoughts, a confusion that her carefully switched-on smile had done nothing to hide. And there, behind the pretence at happiness, was something darker, something Sienna wouldn't have recognised if she'd seen it earlier.

But she knew it now. Now she recognised the shadow of

the same pain she had felt when Keir had walked out on her to go and sleep elsewhere. And blending with the sense of loss was the most devastating thing of all. This was a photograph of a woman deeply in love, but as yet unaware of what she really felt. It was there in her eyes, in the yearning that she hadn't been able to conceal, the need that was etched onto her face.

'Oh, *no*!'

Sienna's hand clenched over the photograph, crushing it impossibly. When had this happened to her? *How* had it happened to her? How could she have fallen in love with Keir when she had been so totally convinced that she'd loved Dean? And yet now, somehow, what she had felt for Dean seemed so alien, unfounded, light-years away from the way Keir made her feel.

So what made the difference? Sienna started the car, manoeuvring it out of the parking space with far less than her usual attention to what she was doing. Her mind was whirling, struggling to cope with the conflicting memories and emotions her heart was throwing at it, forcing her to look at them squarely in a way that she had never done before.

'Believe me, if I could have what I *really want*, you wouldn't be the man with a wedding ring on his finger!'

Her own words, spoken in anger on her wedding day, came back to haunt her.

'And if I was to achieve a *dream*, then I would have married—'

I would have married Dean. That was what she had meant. She had thought herself in love with Dean. Believed that his cruelty, his faithlessness had broken her heart. So how could her affections have swung from one man to another, with barely so much as a heartbeat in between?

Because she had never truly loved Dean.

The truth dawned with the effect of a blow to her head, making her stall the car at traffic lights, earning her a reproachful blare of the horn from the driver behind her. Moving off hastily, she drove on automatic pilot as reality finally took the place of the self-delusion she had suffered from for so long.

Dean had set himself to win her over. He had been unfailingly pleasant and cheerful, always apparently kind, considerate—always so damn *nice*. He had never been impatient, never angry, always gentle, always agreeable. And he had always been *lying* to her, manipulating her with charm into getting her exactly where he'd wanted her—in his bed.

Keir, on the other hand, didn't try to be nice. He was always himself, whether his mood was good or bad. And none of it mattered. She didn't need charm or kindness, was indifferent to his temper. She loved being with him no matter what sort of a mood he was in, even when he was cold or downright cruel. And she missed him when he wasn't there.

And Keir had never needed to entice her into his bed. She would have fallen into it without a second thought right from the very start if her mind hadn't been so determined to hold onto her memories of Dean. She had been so ashamed, so confused by the passion she'd felt for Keir, which had been so unlike the gentle emotions she had had for Dean, when in fact those feelings had been telling her the truth about the difference between the two men.

She had been in love with Keir almost from the start. She had just been too blind, too deceived, to see it clearly. She wasn't exactly sure when it had happened, but somewhere along the line she'd fallen totally, irrevocably in love with her temporary husband. Like her mother before her, she'd found the love of her life in Italy, and, like Caroline's doomed relationship, hers too was destined to fail.

But how was she going to face Keir now? Sienna asked herself as she swung her car into the underground parking space beneath the block where Keir had his apartment. She felt as if one complete layer of her skin had been scraped away, leaving her feeling raw and unnaturally sensitive to pain. So how could she face the man she loved and not reveal her feelings?

In the end it turned out that Keir himself had solved that problem for her, temporarily at least, because of—what else?—his work.

'He rang while you were out,' Caroline informed her. 'Some problem at the Belgian depot. He had to fly out straight away. He couldn't say when he'd be back.'

But the reprieve was only temporary, Sienna knew that. Before long Keir would be back, and she would have to continue to pretend that their marriage was nothing more than the business arrangement she had insisted on at the start. There were still almost nine months of the year they had agreed on ahead of her. How could she live through them and not give herself away?

She knew it would be harder than she could possibly imagine. That the layer of skin that she'd felt had been stripped off would never grow back again. That, as a result, a simple look from Keir's dark eyes, a touch, the softest kiss, would leave her feeling painfully bruised. She would never be able to settle in his company. Her mind would be split into two, one half wanting to drive her to throw herself into his arms and beg him to hold her tight, never let her go, the other urging her to keep her distance, reveal nothing of what was in her thoughts.

And she would feel herself constantly hanging back, frozen by indecision, unable to make any move one way or another.

It was like coming home to a different woman, Keir told himself with a sense of something close to disbelief. He had only been away for six days, less than a week, and yet when he returned Sienna was very definitely not the wife he had left behind.

Those aquamarine eyes watched him warily from behind the shield of long, luxuriant lashes, and her soft mouth rarely curved into the wide, brilliant smile that turned his heart over inside his chest. She had put a strict curb on all those impulsive little gestures too. No more gentle touches on his arm or his cheek, no tantalising trail of her fingers over the back of his hand that seemed to say she couldn't keep her hands to herself, and which drove him crazy with the flaring hunger for more.

Her speech was quieter too, with fewer of those fiery, provocative moments of defiance that had so delighted him from the start. A week ago she had been like a nervous, half-tamed thoroughbred, one that trusted no man, acknowledged no one as master, but who allowed him and him alone to touch her, as long as he took care not to startle her. But now it seemed that even such a tentative understanding as they had reached had been destroyed at a stroke. She eyed him warily, starting nervously if he came close unexpectedly, and he didn't like the way that made him feel.

By the time his mother-in-law had made tactful excuses about needing an early night and left them alone together he was definitely spoiling for a fight.

'What is this?' he demanded, hiding unease with impatience. 'What are you sulking about?'

'Why would I be sulking?' Sienna asked, at last showing some spark of the woman she had been a week before.

'Perhaps because I've been concentrating too much on my work? Because I've been away…?'

'It doesn't trouble me at all,' she returned, with an indifferent shrug of her slim shoulders.

'It did before I went,' Keir reminded her pointedly. 'You said you were concerned. . .'

'I said my *mother* was concerned. As a matter of fact, I've been far too busy organising the move to even notice you weren't here.'

Not true! Her conscience reproached her sharply for the blatant lie. She had missed him desperately every single second he had been away.

'Is that a fact?' One dark, mockingly lifted brow questioned the vehemence of her retort. 'Well, that takes care of the days, I suppose. But what about the nights?'

Keir's voice had lowered to a sexy, smoky whisper that

coiled beguilingly around senses already beleaguered simply by having him so near. After the desert of empty days that had passed since she had last seen him, his presence had thrown her responses into sensory overload. She felt like someone who had been starving and was now suddenly presented with a banquet, and didn't know which course to concentrate on first.

If she looked into his eyes, she couldn't see the hard, lean strength of that stunning body. If she let her gaze dwell on the width of his shoulders, the strong wall of his chest, she missed the softness of his mouth, the smooth silk of his hair. She wanted all of him, every glorious, stunning inch, and yet fear of betraying herself and revealing the force of her feelings forced her to impose a distance that was the last thing on earth she wanted between them.

'The nights?'

She aimed for airy unconcern and almost managed it. The nights had been the worst. She had been unable to sleep for hours, lying awake lost and desolate, supremely conscious of the empty space beside her, the inanimate cold of the sheets where there should have been the living, breathing warmth of Keir's body.

And when at last exhaustion had overcome her she had drifted into a restless, unsettled doze. Her shallow, unsatisfying sleep had been filled with burning dreams, dreams filled with heady, erotic images of Keir, of his kisses, his caresses, and the blazing, scorching passion that they lit in her responsive body. She had tossed and turned, waking drenched in sweat and with her body aching, crying out for the fulfilment it longed for and for which her wanton dreams were no possible substitute.

'I got some decent sleep at last,' she managed, with a dark flippancy that she hoped hid the bitter reality from him.

'Did you indeed? Then you'll be well rested.'

'And just what is that supposed to mean?'

His sigh was a masterpiece in its balance of resignation and exasperation.

'What do you think it's supposed to mean? Perhaps foolishly, I had hoped, in the depths of my cesspit of a mind, that you might be glad to see me back. That you would be happy to welcome me…'

She was. Oh, but she *was* glad to see him. And how she wanted to offer him the sort of welcome she knew he meant. But fear held her back. Fear of betraying herself, of letting her new-found feelings show.

Her love was the last thing Keir wanted from her. He had agreed to a no-strings, purely business deal, and any emotion could only complicate matters immeasurably. He was her husband for the year only, and when the time was up he wanted to go, be set free to walk away without a backward glance.

'So I'm going to have to work a little harder, am I?'

The casual way Keir slipped his hand into the pocket of his jacket deceived Sienna completely. She had no sense of anticipation, no suspicion at all. And when he waved his fingers under her nose she stared in total incomprehension at the beautiful piece of jewellery that dangled from them.

The gold bracelet was the most delicate piece of work she had ever seen. Each link was made up of a tiny flower at the heart of which, brilliant as a dewdrop, glistened a perfect, dazzling diamond.

'An early Christmas present for my beautiful wife.'

'Keir!' Sienna breathed in shock and disbelief. 'I don't know what to say! You shouldn't have!'

Until Alexander's was secure, he should be ploughing all his money back into the company, not wasting it on extravagant fripperies for her! But as Keir dropped the bracelet into her upturned palm and closed her fingers over it she couldn't suppress the rush of excitement and delight that came from knowing he hadn't completely forgotten her while he had been away. He had thought of her. And he had taken the time to select this lovely, perfect gift.

'Oh, Keir!' Impulsively she pressed her lips against the

lean plane of his cheek. 'You're so generous! I don't know how to thank you!'

'Don't you?' he questioned huskily, the dark fires in his eyes blazing down into hers in an eloquent declaration of intent. 'Well, this will do for a start…'

His arrogant dark head swooped down and the hard, confident mouth captured hers, his kiss a demand more than a caress as it crushed her lips beneath his. It took just the space of a single, jolting heartbeat for that kiss to light the fires already smouldering in her heart, melting away any thought of resistance and setting her blood thundering through her veins.

Keir parted her lips to invade her softened mouth, thrusting, tasting, demanding, communicating without words the fierce, impatient need that had him in its grip. His urgent appeal to her senses cut straight through what remained of her defences, pushing her into an open, yielding admission of her own desire. She trembled hungrily beneath that devouring onslaught. It made her feel wanted, dominated, and weak with hunger.

Her hands snaked up to coil around his strong neck, shaking fingers tangling in the crisp, short hair at the nape. An instinctive, sinuous movement of her hips against his brought her into close contact with the heated force of his erection, taut against the close fit of his perfectly cut trousers. She had no way of knowing whether her moan of need preceded Keir's or vice versa, only that the two blended together into a single sound of longing.

'Upstairs?' Keir muttered roughly against her ear, his voice thickened and rough, a flare of heated colour searing his strong cheekbones.

'Upstairs,' Sienna whispered in confirmation, unable to find the thought to form any further words.

They weren't needed. Keir looked for no further encouragement, instead swinging her up into his arms and carrying her bodily towards the stairs.

'If you knew how I've missed you!' Keir declared huskily

as he tumbled her onto the bed to lie in a splayed heap of limbs. He gave her no time to adjust her position, coming down beside her and tugging impatiently at her clothes.

For once he seemed to have lost all his finesse as a lover, too aroused, too ardent to take his usual care in easing her clothing from her. But Sienna welcomed this new clumsiness as she had delighted in that unevenly voiced 'I've missed you.'

With her own love so desperately close to the surface, needing only the slightest urging to come tumbling out, she revelled in even the slightest hint from Keir that he too was more emotionally involved than before.

'Keir…' she whispered shakily, the longing for him a tight knot of pain low down in her body.

'I know, sweetheart.' His soft voice soothed. 'I know. It's been a long, long six days, but I intend to make up for that now.'

'Yes… Oh, yes.'

It was a sigh of contentment, cracking in the middle as his hands stroked over her body, making every inch of her throb in intense arousal. She had likened her need of him to an addiction, and now she knew how true addicts felt when, having endured the pain of withdrawal symptoms, they were once again able to feed their craving.

Hard fingers splayed across her spine, crushing her close against the heated length of him, and his mouth seemed to be everywhere, on her hair, her mouth, the wild pulse at the base of her neck, then, hungrily demanding, back on her lips again. And all the while his hands roved over her skin, leaving burning, erotic trails where they touched, making her moan her delight out loud.

Cupping her breasts, he lifted them to his mouth, caressing the hardened buds with his lips and his tongue. But when she would have caught his head in her hands, fingers tangling in the luxuriant dark hair in order to drag his mouth back to hers, he tugged himself gently free. The next moment Sienna froze into stunned stillness, her body arched to meet the tormenting trail of his kisses over the soft skin of her stomach and down to the most intimate spot of all.

'Keir!' she gasped, pushed to too high a pitch to know or care what she was saying. 'Keir, my—'

Realisation dawned just in time to have her swallowing down the incriminating word. *My love*, she had almost said. *Keir, my love!* And the realisation of how close she had come to giving herself away put a new exigency into her caresses, her hands sliding down between their two bodies and closing over the hot, hard length of him. She knew a sense of very feminine triumph as she heard him groan aloud.

'Sienna!' Her name was just a raw, hungry sound. 'Darling, if you do that, I… You drive me wild; I can't…'

'Do you think I mind?' Her own whisper feathered laughter against his ear. 'What if I want you wild?'

Above her, Keir's eyes closed and his dark head fell back, hectic colour burning across his cheekbones.

'In that case, my lady…'

The heated, wild invasion of his body into hers was so intensely welcome that Sienna felt scalding tears spill from the corners of her eyes and trickle down her cheeks. This was the fist time she had truly made love with Keir, knowing that he had her heart, and the heightened pleasure that secret knowledge brought was almost more than she could bear.

'Sienna?' To her horror Keir had sensed the change in her, the dampness of her tears against his face. 'What…?'

But Sienna couldn't bear the searching intensity of his dark eyes. Moving her head restlessly on the pillow, she tried to avoid that probing stare.

'Don't stop!' she pleaded feverishly. 'Please don't.'

And then, when it seemed he would ignore her, when he didn't move but simply looked down into her flushed face, frowning his confusion, she balled her slender hands into tight fists, pummelling them against his strong shoulders in angry reproof.

'I said *don't stop*!'

Taking the initiative herself, she writhed underneath his imprisoning body, exciting herself every bit as much as him. She knew the moment that Keir lost all control. Heard it in the muffled groan of surrender, felt it in the unruly movement of his powerful body. With a raw, guttural sound in his throat, he took up the rhythm she had started and built on it, with a raw, forceful timing that built to a wild crescendo, driving her onwards and upwards until she felt herself explode into a thousand brilliant stars as she tumbled into total oblivion.

A long, long time later she surfaced from the exhausted sleep that had claimed her to find the room shadowed by the darkness of the night. It was as she stirred restlessly, slowly becoming aware of the coolness of the sheets at her side, the empty space where Keir should have been, that the cool, unearthly light of the full moon slid between her half-closed lids.

Forcing them open, she focused blearily on the window at the far side of the room. The heavy velvet curtains were drawn back on one side and Keir, his navy towelling robe pulled on against the chill of the early December night, stood staring out into the darkness, his hands pushed deep into his pockets and his shoulders hunched as if against some unwanted burden.

'Keir?'

His dark head whipped round at the sound of her questioning use of his name, and she smiled sleepily, waving one hand in a gesture of invitation, willing him to come back and join her in the bed once more.

But Keir simply shook his head, and turned back to whatever held his attention beyond the glass.

'Go back to sleep, Sienna,' he instructed quietly. 'You have a busy day ahead of you tomorrow. You need your rest.'

Too tired to disobey, Sienna tried a half-hearted sound of protest, but without any force behind it. Already her eyes were closing once more, warm, drugging waves of sleep reaching out to enfold her.

'Tomorrow…' she managed, surfacing just long enough to catch the faint twist of his beautifully shaped mouth.

'Yes, tomorrow,' he responded flatly, a note she had never heard before shading his words. 'Now go to sleep.'

Turning on her side, Sienna nuzzled her face into the pillow once more, wrinkling her nose in annoyance as a fine strand of hair fell forward, tickling her cheek. It was only as she lifted a lazy hand to brush it away that she realised that the gold and diamond bracelet Keir had brought her, and which she last recalled holding tight in her fist as he carried her upstairs, was now fastened securely around her slender wrist. How…?

But sleep claimed her before she could think of any explanation of its presence.

Hearing her contented sigh, Keir turned once more to study her sleeping face, illuminated by the moonlight that slanted softly across her pillow.

In some ways it had been the homecoming he had dreamed of. But in others it had been everything he had ever feared. Their lovemaking had been so intense, so wild, so unbelievable. And Sienna herself had seemed like a different woman. Herself, and yet not the Sienna he had known up to now.

She had been so passionate, so responsive. He might almost have let himself believe that she had missed him as much as he had her. That the six days apart had made her look at him and their marriage in a different light, so that he could almost imagine there was a future for them after all.

Almost.

If he had fallen asleep when she had done he might have deluded himself completely, seeing what he wanted even though it wasn't there.

But when Sienna had curled up against him, her head resting on his chest, sighing her gratification, he had forced himself to stay awake to enjoy the sensation of having her so close, holding her tight against him. And so he had seen how, as she'd succumbed to the exhaustion that had claimed her, the arm that she had flung around him had relaxed, her clenched fist loosening, fingers uncurling softly.

As she'd done so something had slithered from her grasp, landing in a soft, metallic coil on the warm skin of his chest. The bracelet—presented to her downstairs and clutched in her greedy grasp ever since. An expensive trinket that had brought about a dramatic change in her attitude, transforming it from spiky reluctance to willing co-operation in the space of a heartbeat.

Well, if he left it like that, she might lose it somewhere in the bed, and that would be a pity after the effort she'd gone to to earn it, he'd told himself cynically. And so he'd fastened it round her slender wrist, where she couldn't miss seeing it as soon as she woke.

Face it, fool! Keir now reproved himself angrily, dragging his gaze away from Sienna as she settled back to sleep, and turning to stare into the bleak, cold light of the moon that so perfectly matched his mood. Face the fact that this marriage is still based firmly on commercial lines. With every transaction paid for strictly in hard cash.

CHAPTER TEN

'I HAVE something for you,' Keir said casually. 'Happy Valentine's Day.'

'For me?'

Sienna's head came up sharply from the book she had been reading to stare at her husband in blank confusion.

'But I would have thought that the roses were enough...'

The roses were more than enough. Peach and gold, they exactly matched the flowers in her wedding bouquet, and just to think that he had troubled to remember sent her heart soaring in a singing reaction to his thoughtfulness. She tried not to pin too much on it, but all the same it was impossible not to let herself wonder, to dream. He had been so very generous at Christmas, and now this. Was it possible that perhaps, slowly, Keir was coming to care for her in a way that was more than sexual?

'I still wanted you to have this.'

Belatedly Sienna realised all that Keir held out to her now was a white envelope. Just a card, then, not the extra Valentine's gift she had been foolishly anticipating.

'Well, you obviously don't believe in pretending to be a secret admirer,' she joked as she took it from him.

She had tried that, she recalled, hot colour washing her cheeks. Too scared to send him a Valentine's card that came anywhere near the truth about the way she felt, she had chosen instead one with a jokey inscription and had put it in the post, carefully disguising her handwriting as best she could.

The joke had fallen painfully flat when Keir had opened the card along with the rest of his mail at breakfast time. He had barely skimmed over the words inside, his sensual mouth managing only the faintest flicker of a smile, before he had turned to her with a 'Thanks' so off-hand as to be positively indifferent.

'You want me to know exactly who it's from?' she said now.

'With this, I do.'

Something about his attitude set her nerves on edge. This felt all wrong. It was no light-hearted card for Valentine's Day. Not even a slightly risqué joke, as hers had been.

Sienna's fingers trembled as she ripped open the envelope. It was impossible to hold back the irrational hopes that flooded her mind. Could it be that the roses had just been the start, that they were meant to test the water, so to speak? Keir wanted her to know that this came from him, and so…

Not a card. All the nervous excitement that had buoyed her up left her body in a rush, so that she actually sagged back into her chair. Then what?

It took several more uncertain seconds before she recognised the slip of paper she held as a cheque. Much longer to make out the amount written on it as the figures danced before her eyes.

'What…? I don't understand.'

With a determined effort she blinked hard to clear her blurring vision, forcing herself to concentrate. She recognised Keir's handwriting, the firm, upward slash of his signature, heavily underlined, but nothing else made sense. The value of the cheque was impossibly large, for one thing.

'Keir, what is this?' Shadowed with confusion, her turquoise eyes sought his, meeting head-on a gaze that was dark as jet and every bit as unyielding.

'Can't you guess?' Rough and hard-edged, his tone scraped over already raw nerves, making her shiver unhappily. 'That cheque is for every penny I owe you, plus some extra to cover the interest.'

Every penny I owe you. But why? Afraid to ask the real question, the one that was pounding in her head, she dodged the issue cravenly instead.

'But, Keir—it's so much. Can you afford it?' she asked, affecting a calm she was a million miles from feeling, and finding herself quite pleased with the result. She sounded cool and in control, not the twisting mass of nerves that she was inside.

'Of course I can afford it!' Keir exploded, slamming one fist into the palm of the other hand in a gesture so expressive of his mood that Sienna flinched back in her chair, watching him with wide, wary eyes.

She had known something was up from the moment he had come home. Normally when he got back from the office his first action was to change his clothes, casting off the conformity and restrictions of his work-wear and putting on something more casual and comfortable. But today he had acted completely out of character, keeping on the superbly tailored navy blue suit and matching shirt and tie all through dinner.

Sienna found the formality of his appearance thoroughly disconcerting. So much so that she had found it hard to eat the delicious meal put in front of her. Dressed this way, he looked stunningly handsome, the severe lines of the tailored clothes enhancing the forceful appeal of his lean body, the striking, dark good looks. But he also looked icily remote and intimidating, a sleekly groomed predator whom she watched uneasily from behind the protection of her long black lashes.

She didn't even have the shield of her mother's presence at the table with them in order to dilute the impact of Keir's disturbing presence, deflect the more pointed remarks, fill the most uncomfortable silences. Caroline had found the cold, damp winter particularly wearing, and Keir had insisted that she take a holiday, visiting some friends in Spain, until the weather improved.

'I'm sorry. I didn't mean…' Sienna got to her feet in a rush, feeling far too vulnerable sitting down while he towered over her in this way. 'But, Keir—how?—why?'

The beautifully shaped mouth twisted into a cynical grimace as he lifted broad, straight shoulders in a dismissive shrug.

'How? Hard work, careful investment. Some calculated speculation on the stock market. As to why—well, I'm sure you can guess the answer to that.'

'To pay me back? But the money wasn't a *loan*!' And what did it mean for her, now that he had paid it all off? Where did that leave the two of them?

'I saw it as such—a temporary loan to get me out of an unexpected tight spot. And I knew I'd never rest until it was all paid back. So I took a couple of calculated gambles.'

'Keir, you might have lost everything!'

'It would have been worth it.'

'It mattered so much to you? But why?'

'Oh, come on, Sienna!' It was a low savage growl. 'You understand better than that. You knew I was never going to be a tame lapdog of a husband, someone who would be at your beck and call, come when you whistled. I took your money because I was forced to, I needed it. But I don't need it now, and so—'

'And now?' Sienna prompted nervously when he unexpectedly broke off the angry tirade. 'What happens now?'

Her hands were damp with perspiration, and she wiped them as inconspicuously as possible down the skirt of her deep red, long-sleeved dress. Just what did Keir have in mind for their future?

What happens now? Keir echoed her question in the privacy of his own thoughts. Did he really know how to answer that?

If he was strictly honest, then he hadn't thought things through properly. In fact, he hadn't considered beyond the moment that he handed over the cheque to her. For nearly six months now, all his attention had been concentrated on the prospect of this one moment. The point where he could pay back every penny of the money Sienna had given him and know that, with Alexander's in the clear and the debt he owed to her discharged, everything was on a completely different footing. They could start again.

But nothing had gone as he had anticipated. For one thing, Sienna hadn't even seemed pleased by the gesture he had made. Her amazing eyes had been as cold and unwelcoming as the North Sea on a winter's day, her expression coolly indifferent.

'Have you thought about making this marriage of ours into the real thing?' Keir asked, with a nonchalance that took her breath away. 'After all, we both get on well enough together—and you have to admit that the sex couldn't be better.'

'Is that a proposal?' High and tight with something close to hysterical laughter, Sienna's voice perfectly expressed the disbelief she was feeling. 'Because quite frankly I've had more flattering put-downs! What on earth makes you think I'd agree to any such thing?'

What indeed? Keir was forced to ask himself, shaking his head at his own stupidity. He could only be grateful that he'd managed to hide the way he really felt. This way, he'd asked the question, but without putting himself on the line. He could just imagine what her response would have been if he'd been fool enough to do that!

'Why not?' If he could have managed to sound more detached, he didn't know how. 'Plenty of other marriages have been built on a whole lot less. It's a start.'

'Not much of one!' Sienna used scorn to disguise the pain she felt. 'And what, precisely, would I get out of this marriage you're proposing—other, that is, than a raging sex-life?'

The dreadful thing was that she was tempted! If he had been just the tiniest bit more gentle. If he had couched his offer in terms that were even the slightest bit less insulting, she might actually have said yes.

'A rich husband—because, believe me, Sienna, I *am* rich now. The problems I had are all behind me. A good lifestyle—a child…'

A child. A baby with Keir's dark hair and big brown eyes. Her own private fantasy come true. But she could never admit as much.

'No way! A baby should be brought into the world by two people who truly love each other. A child deserves to have parents who can teach it by example what love is, what it means. They shouldn't just be two people brought together by a temporary difficulty who decided to stay together because they had a great *sex-life*!'

Well, now you know, Keir Alexander! Do you want it spelled out any more clearly than that? *Could* she make it any plainer? Did he really want to stick around and see what little was left of his ego taken and trampled into the ground under her dainty, arrogant little feet?

'Then there's not much point in continuing with this farce, is there? We might as well call it a day.'

Sienna felt all the blood drain from her face, leaving it cold as ice. Twice she opened her mouth to speak, only to have her voice fail her at the last moment. With a struggle, she tried one more time.

'You—you can't mean that!'

He couldn't! Not now. Not yet. Cold and callous and totally unfeeling he might be, but he'd stolen her heart, and if he walked out of the door he'd take it with him, leaving just a raw, gaping hole where it should be.

'I mean it,' Keir returned dangerously. 'Every damn word.'

He was turning towards the door as he spoke. He had every intention of carrying out his threat unless she did something drastic. But what? Desperation forced inspiration into her panicked mind.

'Well, that's just typical!' she flung after him. 'Typical male selfishness! Now you've got everything you want, you don't even spare a thought for me!'

It stopped him at least. Froze him halfway across the room, before slowly swinging round to face her again.

'Everything—' he began, but she was too distraught to

let him speak. Instead she rushed on, the words pouring out of her, totally beyond her control.

'You know what my situation is! How I have to convince my uncle this is real! I must stay married to you or I'll lose everything!'

And he would never know just how true those words really were. Without Keir she would never inherit the rest of her father's money, but then without Keir she wouldn't care about anything like that at all. Nothing would have any meaning.

'If the money matters to you that damn much, I'll give it you. I told you, I'm rich...'

'It's not just the money!' Was he so desperate to be free of her? 'There's this house—my mother's home—and how do you think people will talk if you walk out on me now?'

'By "people" I presume you mean your precious Dean Hanson?'

Dean had never even crossed her mind, but it would be safer not to admit that.

'You owe me a year! That was what we agreed on! I want that year—no more, no less! As I said before, that money wasn't a loan! I—bought you—paid for you...'

She was saying all the wrong things, she knew that by the black, savage scowl that had descended on his stunning features, the blaze of yellow fury in the depths of his eyes.

'The hired husband.' Bleak cynicism lashed at her like the cruel flick of a whip but she forced herself to ignore it.

'You agreed to stay for twelve months, not six. You must stay!'

'Must?'

Must was quite the wrong word to have used.

'You—you promised...'

Abruptly Keir's mood changed. The tension in his shoulders vanished, leaving them with a disturbingly despondent slump as he raked both hands through the dark silk of his hair in a gesture of angry frustration.

'I promised,' he echoed flatly. 'And I should keep my promise.'

He couldn't summon up any emotion to inject into the words. The emotion was all in his heart. How in hell was he to stay in the relationship feeling as he did and knowing there was no hope of a response? How was he to survive when he could only get in deeper and deeper, as the past months had already proved to him?

He'd thought he could have it all. Keir almost laughed aloud at his own foolishness. The company and the marriage. But nearly six months down the line Sienna showed no sign at all of coming to care for him. If anything, she was further away than ever.

But he had promised, and, recognising an Achilles' heel when she saw one, Sienna had gone straight for it. He would never renege on a promise and she knew it. So now he was caught, trapped into living with a woman who saw him only as the key to the money she would inherit. When the year they'd agreed on was up and he'd outlived his usefulness to her she would let him go without even waving goodbye. The real problem was whether he could last another six months without betraying himself. Without her finding out what he really felt.

'All right, Sienna, you win. I'll stay.'

All right, Sienna, you win. He was conceding defeat, Sienna told herself. But if she'd won, why did it feel so much like a total failure? Why did she feel so despondent, so totally desolate, as if something very special, something precious and valuable had just died right there in front of her eyes?

Because she'd won the battle but lost the war. She'd persuaded Keir to stay, but so much against his will that he must always hate her for it. She had used moral blackmail on him, left him with no alternative, and he would never forgive her for that. He would stay because he was obliged to, but he would resent every second he spent with her.

And when the year was up he would escape, throw off

the bonds that he saw as forcing him to be, in that detested phrase, the hired husband and leave without a backward glance. And she would have to let him go. She had no reason to justify keeping him with her any longer. Just to think of it made her heart ache as if it was bruised.

When the year was up! Sienna had to force back the cry of distress that almost escaped her, biting down hard on her lower lip to keep herself silent. The end of the year might be the least of her worries. The real problem was whether she could survive the next six months or so and keep the truth of her feelings for Keir hidden all that time.

CHAPTER ELEVEN

SIENNA wasn't asleep when Keir finally came to bed, just half dozing. But when she felt the bedclothes lift slightly, the bed dip under his weight, and the warm, intensely personal scent of his body coil around her she came wide awake at once. For a few moments she lay absolutely still, wondering whether to speak or take the more diplomatic route of keeping quiet. The past weeks had been hard enough. Was she about to make them more difficult for herself?

In the month since Valentine's Day, it had seemed as if Keir barely existed in her life. If it hadn't been for the fact that he came home every night, then she would never have seen him. He was out early in the morning, often before she even woke, and he stayed out all day, only reappearing later than ever before, often only just in time to collapse into bed and fall fast asleep.

But she knew that he no longer needed to work so hard. Alexander's was going from strength to strength, the investments Keir had made bringing in a small fortune in interest. And so the only conclusion she could come to was that he was deliberately distancing himself from her, staying out in order to avoid having to come face to face with her.

And she couldn't bear it. The few months that were left of their marriage were steadily going by. All around her, the signs of spring's arrival were slowly starting to appear. Before she could blink it would be summer, and at the end of that summer she and Keir would go their separate ways. This was all the time with him that was left to her. She couldn't possibly let it go to waste.

Beside her, Keir stirred restlessly, and, unexpectedly, she

heard him sigh deeply. Just what was the reason for his despondency she didn't know, but she *had* to talk to him—and now.

'Keir?' she said softly, and instantly felt the long body at her side stiffen.

'I didn't realise you were awake.' Coming out of the darkness, his voice was far from welcoming, with no trace of warmth in it.

Not the best beginning, but she forced herself to ignore the tension in him so that she could continue.

'My mother will be back next week. Can I hope that you'll at least make some effort to be home once in a while when she's here?'

Keir lifted his hands and linked them behind his head, staring up at the ceiling.

'So that's what's so important it's kept you awake half the night,' he drawled sardonically. 'Well, you needn't worry your pretty head about things any more. I'll be here.'

He'd be here for Caroline, the moment her mother set foot in the house. But he hadn't been here for her, for his wife, for ages.

'Thanks.'

There was no way she could control her voice. She sounded as ungracious and ill-tempered as a hibernating bear woken far too early from its sleep. And, to judge by the way Keir's head turned swiftly in her direction, he was well aware of the fact.

'You don't sound too pleased with the idea,' he commented satirically. 'Was that the wrong answer? Was I supposed to say, No, I'll make myself scarce so that Caroline will be forced to wonder what's up?'

'Of course not! But that's just what she'll do if you continue the way you've been behaving. Don't you think it's a little too early to start laying preparations so that people won't be too surprised when we finally divorce?'

'That wasn't what was in my mind at all.'

It was impossible to interpret Keir's tone, and the way he

had pulled himself up onto his pillows, leaning back against the bedhead, meant that his face was way above hers, impossible to see. So she had no clues at all as to exactly what *had* been in his thoughts.

'But then I don't think you'd want to know what I was really thinking.'

'Wouldn't I?'

Sienna copied his movement of a moment earlier, levering herself up until she was sitting against the pillows. She caught the flash of his dark eyes, eerie and disturbing in the moonlight coming through a chink in the curtains, glancing at her just once, then away again, with a speed that slashed at her heart in its total indifference.

'And what would you know about it, *husband*?' She emphasised the word with a sarcasm that matched his own. 'When have you been around to learn anything about the way I was thinking? To see anything beyond the needs of that damn company of your—'

'Well, well, what is this?' Keir interrupted her tirade mockingly. 'Are you claiming, dear wife, that you've actually been missing me? That, unlike the last time, this protest is actually on your own behalf and not just your mother's?'

The cynical intonation of that 'dear wife' turned the endearment into an insult that twisted the knife in the wound he had already inflicted on her.

'Don't call me that!' She was beyond thinking if her response was wise, beyond caring how much it gave away. 'Don't you dare use the word wife in reference to me!'

'Why not?' Keir returned with deceptive mildness. Sienna was only too well aware of the way that that ominously quiet voice hid a ruthless temper, only barely reined in. One false move and he would loose his grip on it altogether. 'I understood that was what you are—for now at least.'

Suddenly a fierce, liberating anger filled Sienna's thoughts, obliterating rational thought. She didn't care if she drove him to lose his temper. Perhaps, after all, that was what she wanted him to do. It would be such a change to see some emotion, some passion in him, even if it was only anger. For the past few weeks he had been so controlled, so coolly distant, that at times she had been ready to scream. It would be a relief to let out some of that tension, like hot air escaping from a pressure cooker.

'A wife in name only! A wife who hasn't been treated like a wife! Do you know how long it is since we—since we made love—or did anything together! You're out all day and half the night; I hardly ever see you! If you were a different man, I might think you had a mistress, but I can't even tell myself that! Instead my rival in the…the…'

Desperately she caught herself up as her wayward tongue almost gave the game away completely. *My rival in the love stakes* she had been about to say and her heart clenched in panic at the thought of just how Keir would have responded to *that*!

'My rival for your attention,' she amended hastily, 'is your company!'

Her words died away into the silence of the night. A silence so still and profound that it tugged sharply at her nerves, making her skin feel cold. Say something! she pleaded silently, willing Keir to speak. But still the silence stretched out, tightening her nerves with every fearful beat of her heart. And still Keir said nothing.

She was so tense with expectation of his angry response that when he moved suddenly she flinched away nervously. But Keir had only lifted his hands to rake them through his hair, shaking his head slightly as he did so.

'I had no idea you felt this way. I—'

'Well, what way did you expect me to feel? Was I supposed to sit quietly at home while you were out playing at being the businessman of the year?'

'I was not *playing*!' It came out with a snap from between clenched teeth. 'I was earning the money to pay you back.'

'Money I didn't want!'

That brought his eyes round to her again, studying her so

intently from beneath lowered lids that she shifted uncomfortably against the softness of the pillows. Now that her eyes had grown accustomed to the darkness, she could make out the strong, clean lines of his chest, the wide, straight shoulders, and her fingers itched to stretch out and touch. She had to clench them tightly out of sight under the covers so that they didn't smooth over the skin she knew felt like heated satin, trace the tantalising line of body hair down to where it vanished out of sight under the duvet.

The moonlight played on the carved lines of Keir's face, throwing it into planes and shadows that emphasised the purity of the bone structure, the deep pools of his eyes. Against the immaculate white of the pillow covers, the darkness of his hair was almost shocking. The restless movement of his hands a moment before had ruffled it softly, so that a single wayward lock had fallen forward over the high forehead, just asking to be stroked back into place.

But she didn't dare. His mood was too dangerous, too unpredictable. From wanting the release of his fury, she was now desperate to do anything to avoid it. It was impossible to tell which was worse—the fire of his anger or the coldness of his indifference. Both were brutally destructive in their own way.

'Here we go again,' Keir muttered roughly. '"I don't want...I don't want". Will you ever tell me what you *do* want?'

Oh, but that was easy. If only she had the nerve to say it.

Did she dare? Sienna stared up into the impenetrable darkness of his eyes and drew in a ragged, uncertain breath. Her lips were too dry to speak, and she slid her tongue over them to ease the feeling.

It was as she saw Keir's gaze drop to follow the small movement, the sudden tension in his jaw, that she knew he was not as unaffected by her as he seemed. Was his indifference, then, all just an act? Had he felt the past weeks' separation as badly as she had? Was the hunger that she had experienced even now eating away at him as it was inside her?

'Oh, Keir, don't you know…' A blend of uncertainty and undisguised desire, touched with a hint of soft amusement lowered her voice by a husky octave, and she knew from the way Keir's head went back slightly that he was not unaware of it. 'Surely you can guess.'

His breath was dragged into his lungs with an effort, as if they were raw and uncomfortable.

'Tell me.'

His command was even more rasping than hers had been. The sound of it made Sienna's mood lift dramatically. In this way at least they could still communicate.

With a small smile tugging at the corners of her mouth she finally gave way to temptation. Lifting her hand, she touched it lightly to the strong curve of one shoulder, the smile growing as she saw the shudder he was unable to control. Very gently she trailed her fingertips across his chest, her gaze fixed on the path she was taking so that she couldn't miss the response he fought.

Just for a second she let her fingers rest against the pulse at the base of his throat. Finding it satisfactorily heightened, the blood throbbing beneath the delicate pressure, she let the smile become a grin of triumph. If she couldn't keep him with her any other way, there was always this. Sex had been their way of connecting from the start. It wasn't perfect. It wasn't what she wanted. But it was better than nothing.

'You know what I want, Keir. I want you.'

The breath he drew in was even deeper, rawer, than before. He was weakening. Whatever wounded pride or determination to make his company the best in the world had kept him from her over the past weeks, it was weakening rapidly. The wall he had built between them was cracking apart, coming down brick by brick. A little more encouragement was all it needed.

Her fingers traced delicate, heated patterns down over his

impressive torso, making small circles in the softness of the fine dark hair, feeling the powerful muscles clench and tighten underneath her touch. Her own heart was thudding painfully, her blood heating until it created a fire of need at the most feminine core of her body.

'Did you hear me, Keir?'

His lack of anything to say was surprising. But perhaps he wanted her to carry on persuading him. Perhaps he wanted to carry out this game of provocation to the very limit. Perhaps he wanted her to tantalise and torment him until he could take no more.

'I said I want you.'

Her wandering hands had reached the line of the bed-clothes and she hesitated, then ran them backwards and forwards along the top of the soft barrier, as if debating whether to go any further. Keir was totally still now, he almost seemed to have stopped breathing.

'I want you to—'

She broke off on a squawk of shocked surprise as Keir moved at last. But not in the way she had anticipated.

A hard hand clamped onto hers, strong fingers closing tightly, stilling her teasing movement.

'I heard what you said,' Keir growled savagely. 'But you'll have to forgive me—I'm not in the mood tonight.'

'Not—not in the—' Sienna turned wide, stunned eyes on his face, finding it closed and shuttered, as cold and unyielding as if it was that of a marble statue. 'I don't understand.'

What had happened to the response she had been so sure of? The passion she had believed was just under the surface, needing just the faintest encouragement to be set free?

Not in the mood? Dear God, Alexander, who are you trying to kid? The hunger was like a pain inside him, clawing at him. But he'd been caught that way before and the inevitable kickback had become harder and harder to endure.

Oh, he could let himself make love to Sienna quite easily.

Let himself! He almost laughed aloud at the bitter irony of the thought. It was all he could do to stop himself from grabbing her and throwing her back on the bed and… But it was no longer the same.

The pleasure—the *physical* pleasure—was still there, intense as ever. If anything, it grew more intense each time he made love to Sienna. He was always fully *physically* satisfied. But deep inside was an emotional black hole that was growing wider and deeper with every day of this façade of a marriage that passed.

He hated the way it made him feel. Feared that one day he might weaken and say what he really felt, reveal his heart openly to her. He was afraid that one night, in the throes of passion, or, worse, when he had had rather too much to drink, he might just let down the barriers he'd lived with for so long and tell her that he loved her.

And so for weeks now he'd held back, making excuses. He'd stayed out as long as he could and come to bed later and later, waiting until he was sure that she was asleep. Or he'd protested a tiredness he was far from feeling. Anything so that he could avoid being in bed with her when she was awake. It was bad enough having to endure the long wakeful hours with her warm, soft body curled so close to his, the perfume of her skin filling his nostrils.

'I don't understand.' Sienna's eyes, pale in the moonlight, were sheened with tears she wouldn't let herself shed. 'What is it? Don't you fancy me any more?'

Fancy her! 'Fancy' didn't describe it. He ached with hunger. Wanted her as he had never wanted any woman, and that hunger never eased, was never appeased.

But he couldn't bear the emotional backlash any longer. Couldn't handle the thought that making love meant nowhere near as much to her. That with her it was only physical. That her mind and her heart were not involved in the way that his were. That perhaps she was even comparing him with Dean and wishing he were the man she loved.

'Sienna, I told you I wasn't in the mood.'

If her tormenting fingers wandered an inch or so below the covers she'd soon prove that statement for the outright lie it was. Silently Keir cursed his wilful body for the all too obvious signs it was betraying.

'But you haven't made love to me for weeks!'

Not with his body, perhaps, but in his mind...! In his thoughts he had been with her, loving her, more times than he cared to count. His thoughts had produced the most erotic, most carnal, positively X-rated films for his own private viewing. But the most fantastical element about them had been that in every one of his dreams Sienna had been avowing her undying love for him.

'We don't have to be at it every second of the day!'

'Keir, we're not *at it* any time. And we're supposed to be—we're newly-weds—we're married.'

'Yeah, we're married,' Keir echoed cynically. 'And this is what happens when you get married. Romance flies out of the window. You sign that piece of paper and everything changes. Reality intervenes...'

'But ours isn't exactly the usual sort of marriage. You're not really my husband, are you? And I'm not anything like a wife. It's not even a *real* marriage.'

'You said it, lady.'

If she'd kicked him right where it hurt most, it couldn't have been more painful. But it had had one welcome effect—it had successfully doused his ardour in a second. At least now he would be able to get out of bed and walk away without revealing the lie he had been telling all this time.

And he had to walk away. He couldn't stay. Couldn't talk to her any more. But he had to make sure she didn't come after him.

'Real marriage or no, Sienna darling, the magic's gone out of it. I mean, look at what you're wearing...'

The flick of his hand that indicated the soft cotton of her well-worn tee shirt was arrogantly contemptuous.

'This...' Sienna caught herself up in a panic, painfully aware of the way that she had come close to admitting that, feeling lost and abandoned, she had pulled on the old tee shirt for comfort. 'It's a cold night!' she substituted hastily.

'In a centrally heated house.'

As if to prove his point, Keir flung back the duvet and swung his long legs out of bed with obvious indifference to the chill of the night. Proudly naked, he strode across the room to snatch up his robe and shrug it on, belting it tightly round his waist.

'You can't walk out on me like this!' Sienna protested wildly. 'I won't let you.'

'You can't stop me.' Keir's contradiction was formed in ice.

And before she had time to recover enough from that final cutting comment he was gone.

Left alone, Sienna wrapped her arms tightly round her slim body, as if to hold herself together. Deep inside she felt as if she was falling apart. As if everything that was truly her was crumbling to pieces, never to be put back together again. The pain of Keir's rejection was almost more than she could bear. And it was so much worse because it had been done so coldly, with absolute control, no trace of anger or any other emotion in his voice.

Somewhere along the line she had foolishly allowed herself to become complacent. Because Keir had desired her so much at the start of their marriage, she had convinced herself that he would always feel that way. That if nothing else, the blazing physical passion they shared would keep him by her side for what remained of their marriage. She had relied on that and allowed herself to hope that perhaps in that time there might be a chance that he would come to feel something else, something much deeper.

Now it seemed that both dreams had been trampled in the dust. Keir didn't even want her any more. So she might as well give up.

No! Even as the thought formed in her mind she rejected it. She still had over five months of her marriage left. She would use them to win Keir back to her, one way or another.

It was either that or face the prospect of a future living with a vital part of her cut away.

And passion would be the easier approach to take. If sex was the way to keep him interested then she'd give him sex, sex and more sex. All she had to do was relight the fires that seemed to have subsided from their original blaze to a mere flicker. This grotty old tee shirt would have to go for a start.

Pulling the duvet up over the offending item, Sienna settled down to some serious planning.

CHAPTER TWELVE

'THERE! That should do it.'

Sienna smiled with satisfaction as she replaced her credit card in its holder and pushed it back into her handbag. It could do with a rest. She'd really given it a battering today! But in the end it would all be worth it.

Or at least she prayed it would be worth it. If the full-scale assault on Keir's senses that she planned, with the help of a morning at the hairdresser's and a beauty salon and the contents of the various carrier bags with which she was now laden, didn't work then she had no idea at all what her next move would be. But there would be one; she was determined on that. She was going to win this battle or at the very least go down fighting.

But first she was in urgent need of refreshment. Her feet were throbbing and her throat was dry. She needed a cool drink before she made her way back home.

The wine bar was crowded and noisy, buzzing with a hundred different conversations as Sienna hunted round for a space to deposit her bags. She didn't find one. What she saw instead had her frozen to the spot, turquoise eyes widening in shock, her blood running cold in her veins.

'Keir!' she breathed, her voice shaking.

She'd forgotten that this bar was a favourite of his. Just a short walk from his offices, it was where he and his employees gathered to celebrate a birthday or a particularly successful deal.

But it wasn't any member of Keir's staff who was with him now. It wasn't even a client or one of his friends. Even though the woman seated on the far side of the crowded room had her back to her, Sienna would have recognised her anywhere.

The red-gold hair was unmistakable, as was the tinkling laugh that now sounded through a sudden drop in the conversation as she leaned forwards to take one of Keir's hands in both of hers. And, in spite of knowing it was impossible at this distance, she actually thought she could catch a waft of Lucille's sickeningly sweet trademark perfume.

Keir and his stepmother, here! Sienna's first coherent thought was that she might be seen if she stayed any longer. Keir, at least, with his back to the window, was facing in her direction. If he looked up, glanced this way…

Panic put wings on her heels, and after a couple of moments' frantic pushing and shoving she was once more outside on the pavement, breathing hard, as if she had run a sprinting race.

Keir and Lucille. Keir and Lucille. The names ran like a litany of horror through her mind. Keir and his stepmother, the woman he professed to hate. But if that was the case, then why was he meeting with her secretly like this?

Sienna gave a low moan, swaying back against the wall and closing her eyes in despair. Was this, and not the demands of work at all, the reason why Keir had been out so late so often? Were assignations with Lucille what had kept him away from home? And, if so, what sick sort of a plot had he been hatching all the time—perhaps even from the moment that he'd agreed to marry her?

'Excuse me, my dear…' A concerned voice penetrated the whirling haze inside Sienna's head. 'But are you all right?'

'Oh, yes!' Hastily she forced her eyes open, staring straight into the anxious face of the elderly gentleman in front of her. 'Thank you, yes, I'm fine. Truly I am. I—just felt rather tired. The crowds, you know.'

'That's London for you. Perhaps you should go in here…' a wave of his hand indicated the wine bar behind her '…and sit down for a moment.'

'Oh, there's no need for that!' Sienna assured him, barely suppressing a shudder at the thought. What she should be doing was getting on her way, so as to be well out of sight as quickly as possible just in case Keir and his companion came out of the wine bar on their way home. 'I really have to be on my way. But thank you for your concern…'

She was already moving as she spoke, not daring to look back in case she saw the tall, proud figure of her husband, or Lucille's smaller, curvier form, trim in the elegant cream suit.

On their way home. And what if their destination wasn't separate—two homes—but they were heading in exactly the same direction? What if Keir's plan was to head for Lucille's house… Because he had to be spending all these late evenings *somewhere.*

From some hidden corner of her memory came an image from her wedding day, the lascivious expression on Lucille's face when she had looked at Keir. Once again she heard that double-edged, 'You always did give great value there, didn't you, dearest?'

No, she wouldn't let herself think it. Desperately Sienna hailed a taxi, wanting only to be home, away from the tormenting images that preyed on her thoughts. But of course leaving the wine bar behind did not mean freeing herself from the memory of what she had seen. That pursued her all the way home, and fretted at her thoughts throughout the evening.

And things were made so much worse by the fact that once again Keir was late. Once more it was almost midnight before Sienna heard his heavy footsteps on the stairs.

By then she was in bed. For a long time she had debated with herself the wisdom of staying up and confronting Keir over what she had seen, having it out with him. But in the end reason had won. She didn't know *what* she had seen, did she?

And, even if things were as bad as she feared, surely it was better to stick to her original plan? Even if Keir's attentions had strayed—to his stepmother of all people!—she could still win him back if she just put her mind to it. She didn't allow herself to consider the possibility that Keir's attentions had never *strayed*, but in fact Lucille had been the one he had been interested in—and possibly his mistress—all this time.

'Waiting up for me again, my darling wife?' Keir's drawling voice, blackly cynical and very slightly slurred, challenged her from the doorway.

Dark hair tousled, brown eyes impossibly bright, and with a day's growth of beard heavily shadowing the strong line of his jaw, he looked totally unlike the elegantly groomed businessman she had seen in the wine bar. The wild, gipsyish look was emphasised by the way that his shirt hung loose, his tie unfastened and dangling round his neck, the tailored jacket slung over one shoulder, a finger hooked into the neckline.

'How very devoted you are...'

'And how very drunk you are,' Sienna returned sharply.

Foolishly, crazily, her heart had lifted as she'd realised the state he was in. To have got this drunk then surely he couldn't have had any sort of enjoyable time with Lucille, could he? Or, if he'd stayed with her, then surely he would have been incapable...

'I trust you didn't drive home in that state.'

'I'm intoxicated, not stupid! Of course I took a taxi.' With his free hand he executed a rather wild salute. 'But thank you for caring all the same.'

'It was the other people on the roads I was thinking of,' Sienna returned tartly, reverting to schoolmistress mode in order to hide the sense of horror that gripped her at just thinking of the possibility of that glorious body being damaged in any way. 'I would hate the thought that you'd hurt anyone.'

'Now that's more like it. For a moment there I wondered if I'd got the right room.'

There would be no talking to him tonight, Sienna reflected wearily. He was past listening to anything she said. And, knowing how volatile his temper was these days, even when sober, she wasn't prepared to risk the nuclear explosion that must inevitably result if she provoked him in this mood.

'I wasn't sure if you were in fact my beloved and loving wife…'

'In the flesh, as you can see.'

That comment had been a mistake, she realised, as in response to her words Keir's polished onyx eyes slid downwards from her face and moved lazily over the amount of creamy skin, the flushed curves of her breasts exposed by the black satin and lace nightgown that had been one of her purchases earlier that day.

'And what flesh,' Keir muttered, the words thick with sensual appreciation as he levered himself upright from the doorpost against which he had been lounging. 'Sienna, you look…'

As he paused, seeming to hunt for the right word, Sienna's heart skipped first one then several beats at the thought that the first stage of her plan had succeeded. Perhaps it wasn't quite as she would have wanted it. She would have much preferred it if Keir had been completely sober, so that she would have known his comments came from the heart, but it was a start.

'Devastating…' It was dragged out into a long, aching sigh.

But a second later a change came over Keir's face. His jaw tightened, dark eyes suddenly focusing more clearly, and he drew himself up with an abrupt little shake of his proud head, as if to drive away some unwanted thought.

'What are you up to, darling?' His voice was different too. Clearer, curt, and only faintly ragged round the edges. Evidently he was really nothing like as drunk as he had first led her to believe. 'Trying to tempt my jaded appetites?'

The pain burned like acid in her heart. From being what she had wanted so desperately, the desire she saw smouldering in his eyes was now like an image from a nightmare. She had longed for this, dreamed of his finding her desirable and wanting to make love to her, but not like this. Not like this!

'Keir, don't!'

'"Keir, don't!"' he echoed, bleakly mocking. 'Oh, now I know that you really are my wife. Now…'

She couldn't take any more. 'Are you coming to bed or not?'

For the space of a long, drawn-out heartbeat, he paused, narrowed eyes searching her face, his gaze seeming to scorch where it rested. Sienna felt as if her heart was beating high up in her throat, pounding painfully against the tangled knot of feelings that had gathered there, choking her.

Then, just when she knew she could take no more, he shook his head again, more slowly this time.

'No,' he pronounced, slow and deep and inflexible, turning a look of violent antipathy on the inoffensive divan on which she lay. 'No way. Not in *that* bed, not tonight. If I'm to sleep at all tonight—and it's really rather important that I do—I'll have to—'

'Why?' Sienna questioned, interrupting him. 'I mean, why is it important that you sleep tonight?'

'Oh, didn't I tell you?' It was impossible to tell whether his surprise at her question was affected or genuine. 'I'm driving one of the lorries to Carlisle tomorrow morning.'

'A lorry! But why?'

'There's no one else. This flu epidemic has had drivers going down like flies. This consignment has to be delivered tomorrow without fail, and I was the only person available with the necessary licence.'

Or it was another excuse to avoid spending time with her.

'I'm coming with you!' The impulsive words were out before she had even fully formed the thought of uttering them.

'No.' Flat and hard, the single word brooked no argument. He didn't want her with him; resistance was etched into every line of his strong face

Sienna simply ignored it. '*Yes!* Oh, please, Keir! I've never been in one of those huge cabs and I've always wanted to...'

When she turned those huge, pleading eyes on his face like that it was impossible to refuse her anything, Keir thought despairingly. If only he was a little more sober he'd be able to think of some argument against the idea, say something that would put her off.

'*Please!*'

'I'm leaving at six.' His back was against the wall and he knew it.

'I'll be there.'

'This is fun!' Sienna couldn't contain her enthusiasm. 'It's amazing being so high up like this. You can see for miles.'

Keir couldn't hold back a swift grin in response to her exuberant gesture, which took in the expanse of rainswept motorway visible through the huge windscreen of the truck's cab.

'I can still remember the way I felt the first time I drove one of these on my own. It felt like being at the wheel of a tank.'

If he was honest, he had never expected that Sienna would manage to get out of bed to join him in the early dawn, particularly when the weather was so foul. But she'd surprised him by being up and ready by the time he'd made it downstairs.

One look at her determined face had told him that there was no point in trying to dissuade her from coming with him, and anyway he hadn't had time to argue. He'd already been running late, and it had been easier simply to go along with her resolve to accompany him. There was nothing he could do but make the best of it. At least the concentration required in handling the heavy vehicle in the unpleasant weather conditions distracted his attention from the way her tight jeans hugged the rounded shape of her bottom and hips, and the turquoise cotton sweater echoed the colour of her eyes.

'I never realised you actually *drove* for the company. I've always thought of you as management.'

'It was a matter of necessity at the beginning. Alexander's was so run-down that we just weren't making enough to pay the number of drivers we really needed. I got my licence as soon as I could, and went out on the road with the rest of them until things got better.'

'And you enjoyed it.' Sienna didn't disguise the surprise she felt. She was discovering a new and very different side to this man who was her husband. A side that she had never dreamed existed.

The man sitting beside her in the cab, casually dressed in an elderly grey sweatshirt and black jeans, strong fingers firm on the wheel, every movement sure and confident and in control, was light-years away from the sophisticated, immaculately groomed businessman she had thought she was married to.

This Keir seemed years younger, his brown eyes alight with something close to excitement, the long body relaxed and yet always alert, ready to cope with any problem that presented itself. He looked powerfully, vibrantly alive, vital energy crackling through him, seeming to play around him like an electrical storm. And Sienna felt herself caught up in his enthusiasm with him.

'I loved it. Loved the freedom, the hours—days—when there was just me and I didn't have to answer to anyone else.'

'Was that so important to you? I thought you got on well with your father.'

'With my father, yes.'

The emphasis on the word 'father' brought Sienna's head round to stare at him, a faint frown creasing the space between her brows.

'But not with…?'

The sudden memory of the scene in the wine bar the previous day made her tongue falter nervously, fearful of the repercussions if she actually framed the question. But Keir supplied the remainder of the sentence, completing it with surprising equanimity.

'Not with my stepmother—or my own mother, for that matter.' His mouth twisted into a cynical grimace. 'I never seemed to be able to manage any sort of a real rapport with the female side of my family.'

Which was such a loaded comment that it had Sienna moving restlessly in her seat, painfully aware of the way it could be made to apply to her. But her courage failed her at the thought of questioning him further on either that or the subject of Lucille, and so, acknowledging her cowardice, she stuck to the least contentious topic.

'You didn't have an easy relationship with your mother?'

'That is very definitely an understatement, my dear Sienna. No one had an *easy* relationship with my mother; she was a very demanding woman. Just because she died appallingly young, it didn't make her a saint. At times she made my father's life hell with her unceasing complaints, her extravagant spending—'

Keir broke off in order to concentrate on manoeuvring the truck around a roundabout, but when they were once more back on the straight road he continued as if his speech had never been interrupted.

'That was why the company was in such bad shape when I left university—the money she took out of it, and the fact that my father completely went to pieces after she died. It took us years to pull things round again, and I'm sure the stress of those times took their toll, contributing to the stroke that finally killed him.'

Keir's expressive mouth twisted sharply again, revealing his feelings only too clearly.

'The only thing I can say is that at least she was nowhere near as bad as the second Mrs Don Alexander.'

'Lucille...' Sienna's uneasy whispering of Keir's stepmother's name earned her a slanted, narrow-eyed look, swift and assessing.

'Lucille,' he repeated when she couldn't continue. 'What is it, Sienna?'

'I—I saw you with her yesterday.'

At first she thought he hadn't heard her. His face betrayed no response; he changed gear every bit as smoothly as he had done everything up to now. It was only when he expelled his breath on a hiss of exasperation that she realised that the calm he displayed was only on the surface, and what was underneath was far more complex than she knew.

Abruptly Keir indicated left, swinging the truck into the lane that led to the motorway services. It was only when they had parked and he had switched off the engine that he turned to her, his expression icily distant.

'You saw Lucille with me,' he corrected coldly. 'Not the other way around. There is a difference.'

She wanted desperately to believe him. Everything in her heart cried out to accept his version of the story and so ease one of the causes of the unhappiness that she had endured for the past weeks. But was she being gullible and naïve to let her emotions rule her head? Uneasily she ducked her head in order to avoid that intently probing, dark-eyed gaze.

'She was holding your hand…' she muttered, unwillingly to give him an easy victory.

'Exactly. *She* was holding…' with a suddenness that made her jump, Keir reached out and closed his hand over Sienna's, where they lay in her lap '…*my* hands… Do you see?'

And of course she did. Looking down at Keir's strong fingers folded over hers, in exactly the same position as Lucille's had been, she could recall only too clearly how the older woman had reached for Keir in much the same way as he had just demonstrated to her. Though that still didn't mean their meeting was totally innocent. Still unable to meet his eyes, she could only nod in silent acknowledgement.

'Sienna.' Keir's voice was suddenly surprisingly soft, gently cajoling her out of her withdrawn mood. 'Could it be that you were the tiniest bit jealous?'

But that would be admitting too much. With a jerky, peevish movement, Sienna snatched her hands away from Keir's, pushing them restlessly through her hair.

'And why exactly would I to be jealous of her? It's not as if she's got anything I want…' Or anyone, if Keir's story was to be believed. 'Seeing as we've stopped here, have we time to have a drink? I'm dying for a coffee.'

She waited only long enough to see his curt nod of agreement before opening the door and clambering down from the high cab. Keir was close behind her as she marched towards the coffee bar. In the queue to buy their drinks he was a dark, silent figure whose presence lifted all the tiny hairs on the back of her neck in instinctive awareness, but he didn't say a word until they were actually seated at a table inside the café. Only then did he turn to her, a frown drawing his dark straight brows together.

'I'm having trouble believing that you could actually think I would make a secret assignation with Lucille…'

'Did I mention secrets—or assignations?' Sienna tried for flippancy, praying that her expression, the anxiety in her eyes, wouldn't give her away.

'You didn't have to.' Keir was stirring sugar into his coffee with unnecessary force. 'It was all written there on your face. You thought I'd arranged to meet her…'

'You didn't?' It came out too quickly, destroying her earlier pretence at carelessness.

Keir looked deep into her troubled turquoise eyes, his expression unexpectedly serious.

'No, I didn't. Look, Sienna, let me tell you a few home truths about Lucille. About this woman who you choose to believe I would dally with at the risk of yet more damage to our marriage…'

'Choose to!' Sienna protested indignantly. 'You make it sound as if I'm looking for—'

'Well, aren't you? Sienna, I made a commitment to this marriage when we first started out on it. A husband for a year was what I promised, and I have no intention of putting that in jeopardy.'

It was truly terrifying how easy it was to believe him. When those dark eyes held her mesmerised, and his voice rang with conviction, he could have told her *anything* and she would have accepted it. The noise and bustle of the café around them blurred to an indistinct haze and in that moment it seemed as if there was only herself in the world with Keir, this man she loved so desperately and yet dared not tell.

'Lu—Lucille…?' she managed to remind him, in a voice that sounded raw and husky, as if from overuse.

'Lucille,' Keir repeated, scowling darkly. 'The woman who broke my father's heart but wouldn't let him go. She didn't want him, but she wanted his income, and so she clung like a limpet to that marriage certificate even after it ceased to have any meaning whatsoever. She had numerous affairs when they were married, bled him dry with her spending. And even when he was dead she didn't let go, but lingered like a vulture, picking over what was left.'

He picked up his coffee cup and drank from it, but Sienna was sure that he never even tasted the dark liquid.

'Legally she was still his wife, and as he'd never got around to changing his will when she ran out on him, she was entitled to everything he'd left her. And that was to have been her last revenge. She knew exactly to the penny what I had available to buy her out, and so she asked for that plus half as much again. If I didn't pay she would sell to someone else, and Alexander's—the company Dad had put his life into—would be no more. I was desperate.'

So desperate that he had taken the offer *she'd* made to him. He'd signed away his freedom for a year in order to save Alexander's in his father's memory.

'Keir…' Sienna's eyes were soft as she looked at him, seeing the proud head downbent, that dark gaze staring broodingly into his coffee cup. 'You don't have to tell me this.'

That brought his head up sharply, brown eyes blazing into sea-green.

'Oh, but I do. Don't you see? I want you to know that nothing on this earth would force me into meeting with that she-wolf ever again. That if she hadn't come up to me in that wine bar yesterday and—'

He broke off abruptly, shaking his dark head as if to rid himself of the memory.

'I would never have sought her out.'

Sienna felt as if her emotions were on some violent out-of-control seesaw. Just as her heart was soaring in delight, hearing the vehement conviction of his declaration, a tiny, more rational part of her mind noted a disturbing tension about Keir's shoulders and jaw, an unexpected wariness in his eyes. She was seized by the sudden conviction that he was holding something back. Something vital to her peace of mind.

But she didn't have time to go back over their conversation and try to place exactly when the change had first come over him. Because Keir's next words drove every other thought from her mind.

'You have to see that I would do *anything*—anything at all—to get Lucille out of my life for good.'

Which was a real backhander, Sienna reflected miserably, fighting to force back the bitter tears that burned in her eyes, refusing to let them fall. Because in the same moment that Keir had given her peace of mind on the subject of his meeting with Lucille he had also blasted apart any chance of hope she might have had on another, far more important matter.

'I would do *anything*—anything at all…' Even, it seemed, accept Sienna's proposal of marriage.

Just when it had seemed that she was beyond feeling any more pain, it was clear that Keir could still find new ways of twisting the knife in even deeper.

CHAPTER THIRTEEN

'I NEVER realised that Carlisle was so close to the Scottish border!'

Sienna was studying the book of maps she had discovered amongst the collection of bits and pieces in the cab.

'I've never been to Scotland—do you think?—could we...?'

'I can take a hint!' Keir's tone was dry but suprisingly mellow. 'Yes, we can make a trip over the border, just to say you've been.'

'Great!'

As the day had gone on she had found it increasingly difficult to maintain the level of bright, inconsequential chatter that she had decided was the best way of hiding from Keir the real way she was feeling inside. But this new discovery made things rather easier, and Keir's unexpectedly easygoing mood helped immeasurably.

'What's the nearest place in Scotland I might have heard of?'

'Gretna. It's just over the border.'

'Gretna Green?' Sienna consulted the map again. 'Oh, yes... Is it as romantic as it sounds?'

'Romantic?' Keir's laughter was a sound of pure cynicism. 'You can forget any delusions you have on that score. It's pure commercialism through and through. Oh, don't look so disappointed, darling, I'm sure a believer in true love like you will be able to find some romance in the place somewhere.'

It was so loaded with hidden significance that it was like an actual blow to her stomach, leaving her incapable of breathing for a moment. But she couldn't get her mind round what exactly Keir was driving at.

'True love?' she questioned uncertainly, her heart racing in double quick time. Did he know? Had he guessed? How—*how*—had she given herself away?

'Oh, come on, sweetheart! You must be the last of the really great romantics. After all, you've held on to your precious Dean's memory all this time...'

'Dean!'

The rush of relief was so intense it was like pure adrenaline, making her head spin.

'You mean *Dean*!'

'Of course.' The look he slanted in her direction was swiftly assessing, his frown revealing the danger she was in, how close she had come to blasting her whole subterfuge wide open. 'Who else?'

Who else!

Sienna took a deep breath, knowing she had to go for broke. She had to find something to tell him in order to distract that calculating mind from thinking back over her reaction, putting two and two together and coming up with an answer that would destroy the balance of their relationship for ever. And she had to make it good.

There was only one thing for it. The truth. Or at least a part of it. Enough to convince Keir and make him stop questioning her.

And besides, she wanted him to know. Wanted it all out in the open once and for all.

'Let me tell you about Dean,' she said carefully. '*Everything* about Dean.'

'Everything?'

Keir's eyes were on the road, but Sienna could tell that every nerve in that long, lithe body was attuned to her, his mind concentrated on her words.

'Yes, everything! It's not a pretty story—and not one I'm proud of. You see, I was duped, deluded—conned. Dean Hanson was a liar and a cheat, a deceiver through and through, but I let him trick me. I was easy prey because I was stupid and gullible and I ignored all the warning signs until it was far too late.'

Bending her head so that the dark fall of her hair hung like sleek curtains around her face, hiding it, she stared down at her hands clasped tightly in her lap.

'I met him at the salon where I worked. He was a salesman for one of the cosmetics firms. We—we hit it off straight away. He was good-looking, witty, charming…' The word tasted sour in her mouth. 'So charming. He told me I was beautiful. That he'd never met anyone like me before. That I'd knocked him off balance in the first moment he'd ever seen me…'

'All the usual garbage,' Keir put in when her voice failed her. 'The sort of thing a guy spouts automatically when he wants to get a woman into bed,' he added sardonically when she turned to him, a question in her eyes.

The sort of thing he would have said to her at the start of their relationship if she hadn't flattened him with the crazy marriage idea. Only with him it would have been true, and not just his hormones talking.

Okay, not *entirely* his hormones talking, he amended with painful honesty. He had wanted her in his bed—fast! The rest had come later.

'The usual garbage,' Sienna echoed in a thready voice that twisted something painfully in his guts. 'Well, I fell for it. Hook, line and sinker. He had me wrapped round his little finger so fast that I didn't know night from day. I was dreaming of rings and wedding bells and happy ever after—and then I found out the truth.'

'Don't tell me. He was married.'

Despondently Sienna nodded, aquamarine eyes dulled and shadowed.

'Married with a kid and another on the way. And…'

Beside her, Keir swore violently as a gear change resulted in a totally uncharacteristic crunching sound.

'There's more?'

'I wasn't the only one.'

This was what she had found so hard to cope with. She couldn't believe that she had been so naïve, so gullible, so totally, senselessly blind. Dean's wife and child had been miles away, but his other woman—apart from Sienna herself, of course—had been right there under her nose all the time.

'Jacqui worked in the salon with me.' It was a cry of pain. 'I saw her every day. Talked to her. Had lunch with her. And I never suspected!'

This time the black savagery of Keir's response, the brutally eloquent stream of curses, made her flinch in the same moment that her heart soared at the thought that at least he cared enough to react in this coldly furious way.

'I was luckier than Jacqui,' she managed, on what was supposed to be a laugh, but one that broke painfully in the middle. 'She ended up pregnant, and when she told him she couldn't see Dean for dust—what was that?'

The growl of the engine had hidden Keir's muttered words, so now as she turned her pale face towards him, he repeated more clearly, 'I said, you really choose your times, lady.'

'Times?' Sienna frowned her bewilderment, turquoise eyes clashing with deepest brown. 'I don't…'

'Sienna…' Her name was a sound of pure exasperation. 'Do you know what it does to me to listen to you pouring your heart out like that and not to be able to do anything about it because—'

His fist slammed down on the edge of the steering wheel in a gesture of burning frustration.

'Because you have to concentrate on your driving,' Sienna finished for him. 'Don't worry, I understand. I mean, what else could you do?'

'If I could just get off this damned motorway, I'd stop this truck at once…'

The vehemence of his response was startling, the suppressed anger in his tone mixing with some other, inexplicable note to create the emotional equivalent of a Molotov cocktail.

'I'd take you in my arms, hold you, keep you safe. Let you cry out all the hurt until you were ready to face the world again…'

'It's—it's all right. I'm not going to cry.'

Not true! her conscience reproved her. Hot tears were pricking at her eyes, threatening to fall and prove her a liar. But they weren't the sort of tears Keir believed she would shed. Not tears of loss and pain at the way Dean had treated her. Instead they were tears of joy and delight, mixed thoroughly with a strong sense of disbelief at the thought that Keir even wanted to comfort her like this. Just to imagine him taking her in his arms and holding her made her blood sing in her veins.

'I've wept all the tears I'm ever going to waste on Dean Hanson. I'm over him. I'm never going to think of him again.'

I'm over him. Keir had to force himself to keep his eyes on the road as Sienna's declaration reverberated inside his head. *I'm over him.* If she only knew how long he had waited for her to say those very words. And now the moment was here but he had no idea how to react. He *couldn't* react or the result would be a very nasty accident on a crowded motorway.

So what did he do? His hands clenched so tightly over the wheel that his knuckles showed white as he was suddenly a prey to the terrible despondent thought that perhaps, after all, those words had come too late. That the past seven months had already inflicted so much damage on what had only been a very fragile relationship to start with that it would be too difficult to repair it. Certainly it seemed impossible that they could ever think of starting again.

And, to make matters worse, he was developing a headache that was making it difficult to think straight. Wearily he sighed, massaging the back of his neck with one hand.

'Is something wrong?' Sienna was quick to notice his reaction.

'I'm tired,' Keir hedged. 'Didn't sleep too well last night.'

And when he had dozed at all his dreams had all been of Sienna, beautiful, sensual Sienna, her creamy skin flushed with warmth, in the stunning black nightdress she had worn last night. How he had ever managed to stop himself from getting into bed beside her and ripping it from her glorious body, he would never know.

'But it doesn't matter. We're nearly there. Just another ten miles or so and we can stop for the night.'

The night. Sienna, you idiot, you hadn't thought of that!

'What—I mean, where do you normally sleep when you're on the road?'

The grin he turned on her lacked something of its usual megawatt brilliance, but at least it contained genuine good humour.

'In the cab.' His amusement grew at the sight of her stunned expression. 'There's plenty of room, and it's cosy enough with a duvet… But don't worry, I won't expect you to share. I expect you'd find it rather too intimate for comfort.'

If only he knew that intimacy was exactly what she hungered for. But Keir was concentrating fiercely on his driving, so much so that he completely missed the play of emotions over her face.

'I rang ahead from the first services we stopped at and I've booked us into a hotel together.'

'Together?'

Dark brown eyes were slanted in her direction, and in spite of the brevity of that glance she was shocked to see how dilated his pupils were. He looked pale too, worryingly so.

'The hotel only had one room. So I'm sorry, you'll have to share with me tonight.'

There had been no need for that 'sorry' Sienna told him

blithely in the privacy of her thoughts. 'Together' was exactly what she wanted for tonight.

But by the time they finally reached their hotel it was obvious that any plans she might have would have to be shelved. Keir was evidently decidedly unwell. He had lost all trace of colour and it seemed that he could barely open his eyes. His skin was faintly sheened with perspiration and felt damp and clammy under Sienna's fingertips when she touched him.

'Keir, what is it?' she asked anxiously as the lift moved upwards towards their floor. 'Are you ill?'

'Migraine.' His voice was rough and hoarse, as if it came from a painfully dry throat. 'I don't get them often, but when I do…'

The words trailed off and he swayed on his feet.

'Here…' Stepping forward hastily, she took his arm. 'Lean on me.'

The unexpected ease with which he complied, when she had expected at least a token protest, was more worrying even than his pallor. His arm around her shoulders was warm and heavy, and she had to stiffen her back to support him.

The short trip down the corridor seemed to take an age, but at last they reached their room. Sienna had barely got him inside before he lurched to the bed and collapsed face-down, burying his head in the pillows.

'Keir…' It was shocking to see him like this. She had always thought of Keir as being so strong, so capable, someone who could handle everything. 'Do you have any medication? Tablets you can take?'

'At home, in London,' he managed, his voice muffled by the pillows.

Not much use to him there, Sienna told herself. But there had to be something she could do to help. Suddenly inspiration struck.

'I have to go out for a minute, Keir. But I won't be long, I promise. Half an hour at most.'

By a lucky chance she found a chemist still open in the very next street so in the end she was less than half that time. The small pile of discarded clothes on the floor beside the bed told their own story. Keir had just had enough strength to strip them off before subsiding back under the covers.

'Well, that'll make my job easier. Here, take these…'

Compliant as a tired child, Keir swallowed the painkillers she held out to him, opening his eyes just wide enough to eye the two bottles she held with faint curiosity.

'What…?'

'Lavender essential oil and almond oil as a carrier. I'm going to give you a massage. I *am* a qualified aromatherapist, remember,' she added, when he looked slightly sceptical. 'I used to do this for a living. Now lie down on your front so I can do your back.'

Kneeling beside him on the bed, she blended the oils together then poured a little into her cupped hands. When it was slightly warmed she smoothed it over the length of his back, wincing as she felt the tight knots of tension in his muscles just under the surface of the skin. He really must be in pain, she thought in some distress.

Fired by a determination to help, she swept her palms up the long straight line of his spine to the nape of his neck and out across his shoulders, kneading firmly on the taut muscles.

'Mmm…' Keir sighed softly. 'That feels good.'

Already he was beginning to relax a little, something of the strain easing out of him under the pressure of her trained movements.

'Don't stop.'

She couldn't if she had to, Sienna admitted to herself. The feel of the warm satin of his skin under her fingers, the scent of his body combined with the perfume of the lavender gave her a very real sense of pleasure, one that carried a potently erotic charge. She had never been more intensely aware of the strength of the muscles in those broad, straight shoulders, the width of his ribcage, the supple texture of his skin.

She could feel the effect she was having on him and sensed an answering response in her own body. Her breasts felt full and heavy, aching faintly, and her blood heated swiftly, flooding her veins with a golden warmth.

'Sienna…' Keir's voice was barely audible, so that she had to bend closer to hear it. 'Something to tell you.'

'What's that?'

'About Lucille… '

'What about Lucille?' The steady rhythm of the massage never faltered, in spite of the new and disturbing tension she suddenly found she was prey to. She didn't want to hear a word about his stepmother.

'Those affairs she had…'

He was clearly having to make an effort to get the words out. But it was obvious that this was something he wanted her to know, no matter what it cost him.

'She tried it on with me.'

'What?!'

Just for a second Sienna lost her timing, her hands freezing in mid-stroke. But then she collected her scattered thoughts, bringing her attention back to the job in hand. Concentrate! she told herself fiercely. Keep your mind on what you're doing. Don't let him know how upset you are!

'She came on to me. One night when my dad was away. She came to my room wearing just a robe, with nothing on underneath. Said she was tired of Old Alexander, and thought she'd try the young one out instead.'

'But you told her no chance.'

It was a statement, not a question. She didn't even need to think to know that that would have been his reaction. After all, she'd seen enough of his hatred of his stepmother, the supreme contempt in which he held her, and his heartfelt loyalty to his father to know he would never have considered anything else.

'Yeah…' It was a sigh of relief, and under her massaging

fingers rather more of the tension eased from his tight muscles. 'She went then. But I always worried…'

'Worried?'

'That my dad would find out. That he'd believe I'd taken an active part in her scheme. It would have destroyed our relationship. And she never gave up. Even on the day the will was read—and yesterday, in the wine bar.'

'She—*Lucille* sought you out?'

'She still has a contact at the office. Someone who'd told her that I was there every day. She thought that our marriage was in trouble. That she could take her chance. I always suspected that might happen if she even got a whiff of a suggestion of our arrangement…'

The weary voice trailed off, and Sienna wondered if he'd drifted asleep. But a couple of seconds later Keir obviously forced himself back to consciousness again. There was clearly something he still wanted to say.

'Obviously I told her to go to hell…'

It was all he could manage. This time he did fall asleep. Deeply asleep, his breathing even and relaxed, the long body finally at ease.

Not daring to risk waking him, Sienna continued with the massage for a few minutes more, ceasing only when she knew he wouldn't stir when she removed her hands. Easing herself away from him, she pulled the blankets up over Keir once more before lying down beside him, staring up at the ceiling, her mind buzzing. The things Keir had said had given her plenty to think about.

At some point, much later in the night, Keir finally stirred, surfacing from the deep sleep which had claimed him. His headache had gone and he felt totally different. He felt wonderful, he thought, stretching luxuriously, then freezing as the movement brought him into contact with the warm feminine softness of the woman lying next to him.

'Sienna…'

It was just a whisper but it brought her instantly awake, wide turquoise eyes flying open to look straight into his.

'What is it? Are you all right?'

Keir's smile was gentle, warm. If she'd been weak and foolish she might even have described it as loving. She wasn't as stupid as that, but even so she couldn't stop herself from allowing herself the indulgence of savouring the word just for a moment.

'I'm fine. Your massage worked wonders.'

The kiss he dropped onto the end of her nose was soft as thistledown and heartbreakingly brief. It was there just for a second, then it was gone, and her heart cried out at the pain of its loss.

But then in the space of a heartbeat she saw Keir's face change. Saw the sudden stillness, the swift darkening of his eyes. And she knew what he was feeling because it was happening to her, too. The swift awakening of every sense. The quickened beat of the heart flooding every inch of her body with heat. The spiralling hunger that scarcely seemed to be born before it grew to uncontrollable proportions, impossible to suppress, making her move restlessly at his side.

'Sienna...' he said again, but on a very different note this time, one that drew a deep, heartfelt sigh from her because she knew there was now no going back.

Not that she wanted to go back. Ever. This was all she wanted, all she had ever dreamed of. Everything she had ever longed for was right here in this room, in her arms. She was lost, drowning in the deep dark pools of his eyes, and she never wanted to be rescued because this was what she had been born for, and without it she would always be incomplete.

Keir's smile was slow, surprisingly hesitant, his gaze holding her mesmerised as his hands slid over the curves of her shoulders, down her arms, and across to support the soft weight of her breasts against the heat of his palms.

'Can we do this?' he whispered, and the unexpected, unbelievable note of uncertainty in his voice was the last thing she had expected.

'Can we do this?' she echoed softly, knowing with absolute certainty, without hope of salvation, that if they *didn't* she would die, or at the very least shatter into tiny pieces, impossible to put back together again. 'Oh, Keir, of course we can! We're husband and wife.'

Her encouraging smile was crushed under the force of his kiss, and with a sense of having truly come home she willingly surrendered to their mutual passion.

CHAPTER FOURTEEN

SIENNA stared at the calendar and sighed deeply. It didn't matter how many times she checked the dates, it still said the same.

Of course it did! With a despairing gesture she tossed the pen down onto the kitchen work-surface and sighed again. If only she could throw away her worries as easily. But that was impossible, as, deep down, she had always known it would be.

June the twenty-second. In another two months exactly it would be her first 'anniversary'. The first and last. The day that she and Keir had agreed would mark the end of the agreement that bound them together. So what exactly would they be celebrating? A year together or the start of their lives apart?

Just over three months ago they had been in a hotel room in Carlisle. In bed. That night Keir had made love to her as never before. She had been caught up in a whirlwind of sensation, lifted higher and higher, away from all reality, everything that bound her to the earth. She had given herself to him without restraint, without thought of control or hesitation, and he had responded in kind—or so she had believed.

But only the very next day that idyllic interlude had been exposed as the fantasy that it was and she had come tumbling back down to earth, landing with a very definite and very painful thud.

The truth had dawned on—what else?—the morning after. True to his promise, Keir had taken her over the border into Scotland, into Gretna Green. And while they were there a bride had arrived for her wedding. White dress, heather in her bouquet, even a Scots piper walking before her, escorting her to the ceremony.

And it had been as the piper began to play, as the first haunting notes had sounded in the cool spring air, that Keir's mouth had twisted and he had muttered with black cynicism, 'There she goes. Another lamb to the slaughter. The triumph of optimism over reality.'

She'd needed that, Sienna told herself. Needed the cold splash of realism in her face, driving away the last foolish remnants of fantasy that had still clung to a mind so stupefied by passion, drunk on sensuality, that it had been in danger of being unable to see the truth when it jumped up and bit her.

After all, she'd been there before. Hadn't she already had far too much bitter evidence of the fact that, where Keir Alexander was concerned, passion was a substitute for love, not a vital component of it? To Sienna their lovemaking had been an expression of a deeper feeling, of true sharing, and a promise of a more permanent commitment. But Keir had no idea at all of for ever. To him the ardour of the moment was just that, for the moment, and when it was over, having taken his fill of pleasure, he was perfectly capable of turning and walking away.

But for Sienna that could never be. And not just because of the way she felt about her husband. Because the passage of time had forced her to face up to another reality, one she had at first only feared, but now knew to be a definite fact.

That night in Carlisle, for the first time since their marriage, Keir had made love to her without the use of any form of protection, and now she knew just what a mistake that had been. She was three months pregnant by a man who showed no sign at all of reconsidering his determination to end their marriage once they had reached their first anniversary.

Unobserved, Keir watched Sienna from the doorway, his heart sinking as he saw the way she studied the calendar. It was obvious that she was counting off the days to the end of their marriage, and to judge by the expression on her face it clearly couldn't come soon enough.

'Why the big sigh?'

The casual question made Sienna jump like a startled cat, whirling round to face him.

'Oh—nothing! I was just thinking how the calendar says it's summer, but the weather doesn't seem to agree.'

'It's an English summer,' Keir laughed. 'Rain, rain, and more rain. How about if I take you away from it all?' he added unexpectedly. 'Somewhere warm. What about Italy again?'

'No thanks!' Sienna answered hastily. How could she go back to Italy when her memories of that first time, of her honeymoon, were still so vivid in her mind? She doubted if she would ever set foot in that magical country again, because if she did her pleasure would be tainted by images of herself and Keir during those strange, unreal first days of their marriage. Days when she had still been able to hide behind the protective armour of pretending to herself that she wasn't in love with her husband.

'Well, then, what about dinner, at least? Caroline is visiting a friend tonight, so you needn't worry about her being on her own. We could make a night of it. Say yes, Sienna,' he urged, seeing the uncertain, hesitant look that crossed her face. 'I have something very important I want to talk to you about.'

'You do?' Sienna's heart seemed to turn a somersault inside her chest. What could Keir want to talk to her about that he would describe as 'very important'? 'What is it?'

But Keir simply adopted a mysteriously evasive expression, shaking his dark head adamantly.

'Tonight,' was all he would say. 'I'll tell you everything tonight.'

This was how it had been for the past three months, Sienna reflected as she began her preparations for the evening ahead of her. Ever since they had returned from

Carlisle Keir had almost seemed to become a different person. He had changed his behaviour completely.

The long working hours, the late nights were now just a memory. Keir came home every evening; he took every weekend away from the office. But it was more than that. He had never been so attentive, even in the early days before they had married. He took her out—to restaurants, to the theatre, to concerts. And as the days had grown warmer and longer he'd organised outings—picnics, days by the sea, countless special treats. If she had been asked to describe his attitude in a single word, she would have said that he *courted* her.

Except that courting usually led to something. An engagement, or a marriage, and she and Keir already had both of those behind them. All that this change in Keir's behaviour was leading to was their divorce; because never once had he suggested that they didn't stick to the plan she had originally detailed when she had proposed to him, almost a year before.

But she enjoyed this new way of living, and went along with it, making no protests and asking no questions. She welcomed any crumb of warmth, any attention he was prepared to offer her. After the devastating experience on Valentine's Day of thinking that she had lost him, that he was ending their marriage right there and then, she certainly wasn't about to look any gift horses in the mouth.

'Ready?' Keir appeared in the doorway as she was putting the last touches to her make-up.

'Just coming.'

She slid her feet into high-heeled court shoes, smoothed down the rich blue silk of her elegant vee-necked dress, and turned to survey herself in the mirror.

'You look wonderful.'

In the glass her eyes met Keir's, and she saw the warmly sensual approval in their ebony depths. Immediately her heart gave a nervous flutter, like the wings of a dozen butterflies beating inside her chest, as she fought to control her instinctive response to his smile.

Because over the past few months, while her days had been peaceful, warm, filled with unexpected delights, the nights had been so very different. The hedonistic sensual indulgence of the night in Carlisle had never been repeated. Clearly Keir saw it as a mistake and had moved to clamp down on such unrestrained behaviour. Or it had been just the last throes of a passion already waning that had now burned itself out completely?

'You're not so bad yourself,' she managed, with a lightness she was far from feeling.

The sober dark suit fitted his superb physique like a glove, the fine material of his cream shirt clinging to the muscled lines of his chest, its pale colour bringing out the darkness of his hair and eyes. The superb cut of his trousers emphasised the impact of sleek hips and long powerful legs, a narrow leather belt cinching the slim waist. Seen like this, Keir was every inch the sophisticated, successful businessman she knew him to be.

But she had also known, all too briefly, another, very different Keir. A relaxed, more informal man, casual in sweatshirt and jeans, who had driven a powerful truck with easy confidence and evident enjoyment Or the less controlled, more vulnerable man who had opened up about his past, about some of his own inner fears when she had massaged his back. Her heart ached for the loss of those other sides to her husband, carefully concealed once more behind the worldly mask he displayed in public.

And the public Keir was very much to the fore now, as he drove her to a favourite restaurant, encouraged her to choose the dishes she most enjoyed from the spectacular menu, entertained her with the sort of light, witty conversation that had her laughing out loud in delight. In fact he played his role as escort to perfection, so much so that it was not until the very end of the meal, when they were actually preparing to leave, that she suddenly remembered the reason they were out together at all.

'You said you had something you wanted to talk to me about, Keir. Something very important.'

It was as if she had thrown a switch, turning off a light deep inside him. Abruptly his mood changed, all amusement fading from his eyes, leaving them shuttered and distant. The muscles in his face tightened, the smile that had danced on his lips all night vanishing in an instant.

'Not here,' he said, scrawling his signature on the credit card slip with such an aggressive pressure that it ripped through the top layer of paper. 'We'll talk about it when we get home.'

Which was guaranteed to set Sienna's heart pounding in panic, a cold hand seeming to twist her nerves into knots, destroying all her pleasure in the evening. As Keir escorted her out to the car and all through their homeward journey her mind was racing, trying desperately to think back, find out just when she had made a mistake, when things had gone wrong.

Because something had gone terribly wrong. Everything about Keir's withdrawn silence, the stiff, antagonistic set of his shoulders, the tension that held his long body stiff in the seat beside her, all communicated the fact that he wished he was anywhere but here.

And so when they were once more inside the house, and Keir had ushered her into the elegant sitting room with its cool cream and beige décor, she couldn't control herself any longer. Already wound up so tight that if she didn't say something she felt she might actually snap in two, she turned to Keir in something close to desperation.

'Keir, what is it? What do you want to talk to me about?'

He didn't answer her, didn't look at her. Instead he crossed the room to select a bottle of brandy and pour himself a drink. Then, as he was about to replace the bottle, a thought obviously struck him and he turned to her again.

'Would you like one?'

'N-no thanks.'

Sienna's response was distracted. Because in those few seconds something had happened to stop her thought processes dead, and then start them off on a very different track indeed.

When Keir had lifted the brandy bottle to fill his glass she had noted a totally uncharacteristic tremor in his hand. It had been there again when he'd replaced the bottle, making it clatter faintly against the tray.

Keir was *nervous*! And that was something she had never seen before. Something had put him very much on edge, and that simple fact was so incredible, so unexpected that it threw her thoughts into turmoil, making her reassess everything that had happened and come up with a totally new interpretation of events.

'Won't you sit down?'

'Do I need to?'

She tried for a joking tone, saw it fall desperately flat, the unresponsive twitch of Keir's lips into a travesty of a smile adding fuel to the fire of speculation that was now blazing in her mind.

Was it possible that she'd got it all completely wrong? Had Keir not wanted to tell her something dreadful, but quite the opposite? Earlier this evening she had likened his behaviour over the past weeks to the old-fashioned tradition of courting. What if that had been exactly what he had been doing, and now…now…

The idea was too important, too fragile, for her to want to risk tempting fate by actually letting it form, even inside her head. So instead she turned to Keir again, unable to wait any longer.

'Keir, please! What is it?'

Still he prevaricated for a few more long drawn-out moments, taking first a sip from his brandy, then another, deeper swallow, as he came to sit in the chair opposite her. He seemed to be hunting for a way to begin, and that was so unlike the cool, confident Keir she knew, the man who always knew what to say, that it seemed to confirm her happier suspicions, warming her heart.

'Keir…' she prompted softly.

Keir's dark head came up, chocolate-brown eyes clashing with turquoise, and in that moment Sienna's new-found conviction faltered, a sliver of her earlier panic sliding in through a chink in her mental armour.

'I think it's about time we stared thinking about the future. We need to think ahead, decide what explanation we're going to give…'

'Explanation?' Her voice was just a raw croak, total incomprehension clouding her eyes.

'For splitting up.' Each word was clipped, coldly enunciated, falling like controlled blows on her sensitised nerves. 'We need to have some reason to get divorced. Something to tell friends—your mother—when they ask.'

When she had actually come round to expecting exactly the opposite, the realisation of the true horror of reality was like the destruction of her soul. If Keir had reached into her chest and ripped out her heart, it couldn't have hurt any more. Her eyes blurred, there was a sound like the buzzing of a thousand angry bees inside her head, and she knew with a sickening sense of conviction that if she hadn't been sitting down she would have collapsed in a limp, lifeless heap on the thick carpet right at Keir's feet.

'We—I…'

No words would come. None at all. Her mind was just one terrible scream of agony. She had thought—hoped—Oh, God, what did she do now?

'If you like, I'll take responsibility for it.'

Keir seemed oblivious to her distress. He was talking in a strangely distant, toneless voice. It was as if he had embarked on a speech that he knew he must finish no matter what. And he had no intention at all of diverging from the script in any way.

'For…?'

'Grounds for divorce. I'll provide you with just cause—adultery, perhaps.'

'Adultery!' How could he articulate such an appalling word with such a total lack of emotion? And how could he even think of suggesting such a thing?

'It's probably easiest.'

'Ease—' Sienna swallowed hard, trying to ease the painful constriction in her throat. 'Adultery with *who*?' she demanded hoarsely and ungrammatically, and watched in horrified disbelief as Keir shrugged broad shoulders dismissively.

'Someone. Anyone. Does it matter?'

'Oh, yes, it matters! It matters like hell! I have a right to know who you're going to be unfaithful to me with…'

The words tumbled out faster than a racing stream, clumsily tangling up in each other in her desperation to have them spoken.

'I need to know who you're going to involve in helping you destroy our marriage.'

'But we don't have a marriage to destroy. You know that,' Keir stated with deadly calm. 'The arrangement was—'

'I know what the arrangement was!' Sienna yelled, unable to express her misery in any other way. Seeing the swift reproving frown he turned on her, she hastily adjusted the volume downwards as she continued, 'You don't have to spell it out for me. I know what we agreed.'

'Then you'll also agree that we need to start making plans…'

'No…'

She was getting to her feet as she spoke, spinning away from him, unable to look into that cold, emotionless face any longer.

'What? Sienna, what did you say?'

On the mantelpiece in front of her, in a silver frame, was a colour photograph of their wedding day, placed there by her mother. Sienna's eyes flinched away from it, unable to bear the sight of her own wide, brilliant smile, the tall, impossibly handsome man at her side.

Slowly she forced herself to turn and face Keir again.

'I said no. I don't want to make any plans. It's too early.'

'The year is up in two months' time,' Keir reminded her cruelly, emphasising the point by slamming the side of his hand down on the arm of his chair in time with the last three words.

'I know that, but…'

What could she say to dissuade him? How could she hope to change his mind?

She couldn't. If he was so desperate to be free of their marriage, he would break away from her no matter what she did. Wasn't it better to agree, to let him go easily? That way at least they might have some chance of remaining friends.

But, *oh*… A cruel hand twisted her heart, so that she had to bite back a whimper of pain. She didn't want them to be just *friends*.

'All right.' She had to force the words out, but even so he had to strain to hear a voice that was little more than a whisper. 'All right, we'll do as you say. But have you thought about my mother?'

'Caroline?'

For the first time Keir's resolution faltered. His head went back sharply, onyx eyes widening in something close to shock. His movements suddenly strangely jerky, he lifted his glass to his lips, downing what was left in it before pushing himself to his feet and crossing to the tray to refill it.

'What about Caroline?' he asked, the hoarseness of his voice betraying the way his composure had cracked wide open.

It was a further cruel body-blow amongst so many devastating hurts to realise how much Keir cared for her mother. To see in his face his concern for Caroline where there was none for Sienna herself. But that affection was the only weapon she had left in her arsenal, and she was determined to use it against him as ruthlessly as she could.

'Don't you see it would hurt her terribly to think that you could be unfaithful to me so soon after our wedding? It would devastate her to find you so shallow, so selfish. She respects you, admires you… She loves you, Keir!'

'Do you think I don't know that?'

The brandy glass was slammed back down onto the tray with such force that Sienna fully expected to see the beautiful crystal shatter under the impact.

'Do you think I don't know how Caroline feels? But I can't afford to think of her—I have to concentrate on you. On what you want. Otherwise I can't do this. I—'

'Just a minute!'

Sienna's vehemence shocked Keir into a silence that lay thick and heavy around them. Slowly she shook her head, trying to clear her thoughts, before turning to look at him again.

'What did you say?'

Had Keir suddenly changed dramatically, or was she actually looking at a totally different man? Had his face always been so pale, his eyes so shockingly dark? Why hadn't she noticed the way his skin was drawn tight over the wide cheekbones, etching white marks of strain around his nose and mouth? Was it possible that, caught up in her own misery, she had been reading him all wrong?

'What did you say?' she repeated more emphatically when he didn't answer her.

'That I have to do this for you. That—'

'But what if I don't want it?'

She would have thought it was impossible for him to lose any more colour, but now his face was ashen with shock. He took a single step towards her, then stopped, his eyes never leaving her face.

'You—?'

'I don't want it, Keir. I want to stay married to you. I want us to try and make a go of things together.'

The words were hopelessly inadequate to describe the way she felt but she didn't dare to be any more revealing, to expose her true emotions without some idea of what he thought.

'I don't think so.'

Keir shook his head firmly enough, but there was something in his eyes that didn't tally with the emphatic negative. A tiny spark of vulnerability that lit a flare of hope in Sienna's heart.

'It wouldn't work.'

'Why not? Surely we have something special…'

'What? *Sex?*' She had never heard such raw anger in his voice. 'Is that really so very special? Do you think that's all that matters to me? Or that it says anything about the way you feel? Do you think that just because I can bring you orgasm, because I can make you shudder in ecstasy underneath me, that I'm fool enough to believe it means you love me?'

'It's part of it. Keir…' Drawing a deep, uneven breath, she took a calculated risk, her heart clenching in tension as she spoke. 'Dean could never make me feel that way.'

She had his attention now, with a vengeance. But she didn't know how to build on it. The problem was that she was working blind, unable to gauge just what he was thinking. And those dark, unreadable eyes gave her no clue at all.

'Would you stay if I told you I was pregnant?'

She had invested so much emotional importance in the certainty that he would say, yes, of course he would stay, that it rocked her world to see the way he shook his head.

'A child should have two parents who love each other, not two disparate people yoked together purely in name. I'd always be there for any child, Sienna; I'd want to be a true father. I've always believed that I would have to be married to the mother of my child. It was what I *wanted*. But I couldn't force you into something like that. I couldn't tie you to a marriage you didn't truly want.'

And that was when Sienna knew. When she realised with absolute certainty that Keir loved her. That he would even go against his own needs, his own beliefs, if he thought it would bring her happiness.

'You need to be free to find someone to love.'

'But, Keir, I already have.'

The look he turned on her was so numb, so bruised that it wrenched at her heart.

'You have? Who...?'

'Who do you think? Keir, you must know it's you!'

Looking into his handsome face she saw the shock, disbelief, the slow, unbelieving dawning of understanding.

'I know nothing of the damn sort!' he exploded, with a touch of the old Keir that brought a delighted bubble of laughter to her lips.

'Then let me put it into words of one syllable,' she said, at long last having the courage to come forward and take him by the hand. 'I, Sienna, love you, Keir, with all my heart, and if you'll let me I'll be your wife for better for worse, for richer for poorer, for all those other things, if only you'll let me be your wife *for real*.'

The last words came out on a gasp of shock as she was whirled into his arms and crushed close up against his chest. One strong hand came under her chin, lifting her face until her eyes met his deep ones, that blazed with a devotion so fierce and true that any last remaining fears were shrivelled up in the stormy heat of it.

'If you love me, I'll never let you be anyone else's wife as long as there's a breath left in my body.'

With a sigh of pure happiness that seemed to come from the depths of his soul he brought his mouth down hard on hers, expressing his feelings in a way that mere words could never manage. Her head spinning, her legs weakening beneath her, Sienna could only cling to him and respond in kind, willing him to know from her kiss the overwhelming strength of her feelings for him.

When at last he wrenched his lips away they were both

trembling with emotion and need, and she knew that the flare of colour high on his cheekbones was matched in her own face as he stared down into it.

'I really think that we should get a divorce, my love,' Keir said when he finally gathered the strength to speak.

That 'my love' told her there was no way he meant what he had said at all, but still his words confused her.

'But, Keir, why?'

'So that we can start again. So that I can propose to you as I always planned to do. So that we can get married all over again, properly this time…'

'As you always planned to?' Sienna pounced on the part of his impassioned declaration that had surprised her most. 'Keir, are you saying…?'

'That I always meant to ask you to marry me,' he confirmed her suspicions easily. 'Right from the start I knew I wanted to marry you, but I wanted to give you time to get over Dean. And I wanted the problems with the company sorted out too, so that I could promise you a secure future.'

She had never guessed that he felt this way. 'That wouldn't have mattered.'

'It would have mattered to me. I thought I had time. That I could sort out my own problems first and then come to you free of all of them. But then you pre-empted me with your proposal, and I was so afraid that if I said no you'd look elsewhere, find someone else, that I jumped in with both feet. I was arrogant enough to think that a year would be more than enough time to make you come to care for me…'

'It didn't take half that long,' Sienna whispered, resting her head against the firm, secure support of his shoulder. 'I knew I was crazy about you before six months were up.'

'You…? Valentine's Day,' Keir declared perceptively, and Sienna nodded confirmation of his assumption.

'I couldn't let you out of our agreement because I was terrified you'd walk out of my life and never come back again.'

'That was not what I had in mind at all,' Keir told her softly. 'What I wanted was a chance to offer you marriage on equal terms, without my being just the hired husband.'

'You were never that,' Sienna assured him. To her, Keir could never be 'just' anything. 'But if you felt that way, why did you stop sleeping with me?'

'The sex was getting in the way. We were falling into bed instead of talking to each other. Making love instead of loving. I wanted to take our relationship back a couple of steps, so that we could learn to get to know each other properly. And I couldn't bear to make love to you when I thought that for you it was only sex.'

'That I can believe. What I don't understand is why you said what you did that day in Scotland.'

'At Gretna?' Supremely sensitive to her moods, Keir had picked up at once on her train of thought. 'Oh, Sienna,' he groaned, shaking his head in amazement at his own actions. 'If you knew how much I regretted that afterwards. But it was either that or admit the way I was feeling—that I was jealous as hell of that wedding being a real one. The sort of marriage I had always dreamed of having for myself.'

'Well, we can have that now,' Sienna told him, smiling up into his face and seeing the love shining in his eyes, so clear to see. 'We can begin again.'

Keir nodded slowly, his expression thoughtful.

'How do you feel about having a private ceremony on our anniversary? Just the two of us, renewing our vows, making them real and lasting this time, a marriage that will be for ever.'

'I'd love that,' Sienna whispered. 'But only if you don't mind a pregnant bride.'

'I don't mind—' Keir began, then broke off in shock as the impact of what she'd said hit home fully. 'You *meant* it!'

'I meant it,' Sienna admitted, her pale skin colouring in response to the blazing, ecstatic force of his smile. 'So I'm afraid it won't be "just the two of us" for very much longer.'

'Do you think I mind? I couldn't be happier.'

Keir hugged her even closer, pressing his mouth lovingly to the corner of her smiling mouth.

'I lied, you know,' he whispered against her ear, his warm breath feathering over her skin. 'I could never have let you go to find someone else. I wanted you all to myself. I always believed that if ever I married it would be for a lifetime.'

'Oh, Keir…' Sienna sighed against his lips as his mouth captured hers once more and the heated waves of passion washed over her, threatening to drive away all rational thought. 'That agreement we made. Do you think we could extend the contract beyond its original term—say for the rest of our lives?'

'That might just be long enough,' he told her huskily, swinging her up into his arms and heading for the stairs and their bedroom. 'And the rest of our lives starts now.'